A
CARD
FROM
MOROCCO

ALSO BY ROBERT SHAW

A CARD FROM MOROCCO BY ROBERT SHAW

HARCOURT, BRACE & WORLD, INC.
NEW YORK

FOR

Philip Yordan, Philip Broadley, Leo Vala,
Jeremiah Slattery, Donald Pleasence,
Alex Davion, Harold Pinter, Alfred Rogoway,
Irving Lerner, Laszlo Gombos, Richard Hatton,
my brother, and my wife

A
CARD
FROM
MOROCCO

1

"Do you never want to go back?"

"What?"

"Do you never want to go back home?"

Slattery reached for the bottle of Chinchón, pulled out the cork with his teeth, and emptied the *anís* over his grey head.

"If my tongue was long enough I'd lick it out of my earholes."

"What an awful waste."

"Sarsaparilla," said Slattery. "These hairs in my earholes is soaking it up like mandrakes. You can't drink. That's your trouble, Arthur. *I* have directed traffic naked in Beverly Hills."

They had been used to meeting casually, in the darkness, around eleven o'clock, in bars, in the old part of the city, but today, for the first time, they met by appointment out in the midday sun: today they met in front of the Prado, got into Lewis's Alvis convertible, drove up the Generalísimo, and left the city by the Burgos road.

"I've got a head like the inside of the President's ass."

Whether it was the bolero, or the woman with the cakes of soap on the tray strapped to her neck, or the woman at the next table feeding her baby with naked breasts—for some reason Slattery would not eat. Slattery took off his yellow shirt and drank. While Lewis picked at a sheep's head, Slattery drank.

"I'm sayin' I have a head like the inside of the President's ass."

So they left the restaurant, and the Alvis convertible, and wandered miserably through slums, not talking, kicking at tins, until the heat was too much for them, and sweating they pushed through a hanging blind to enter this deserted bar.

3

"I, who directed traffic naked in Beverly Hills, have a head like the inside of the President's ass. I keep photostats to prove it. But I wouldn't show you any."

Through the shutters, springing off white window sills, the sunlight fell into huge shadows, lay there burning, burning the cigarette ends, the olive stones, the bottle tops, the toothpicks, the husks of shrimps and the husks of prawns.

"Why do ya keep suckin' your cheeks in?"

Lewis sighed.

"What's that for?"

Lewis did not answer.

"I'm sayin' what's that for?"

"Such a waste."

"Ain't you gonna buy me another bottle?"

"No, Patrick."

"What's this 'No, Patrick'?"

"No, Patrick."

"Aw come on, it smells in here. I was only tryin' to cool down. It's hot in here. There's no fans in here."

"I see that."

"Listen, when there's no conditioners I sweat. I was only trying to cool down. It's hot in here. There's no fans in here. You English are all the same. Bloody faggots."

"If you're going to generalize I'm going home."

" 'If you're going to generalize I'm going home.' What kind of accent is that? You been doctored or something? What kind of accent is that?"

"Don't be so boorish."

" 'Don't be so boorish.' Why do you keep suckin' your cheeks in?"

"I don't mock *you,* you know."

"You couldn't mock me."

"You should hear me." This time Lewis barked—he lowered his chin, he lowered his pitch. He spoke as Slattery would have spoken.

"Go on."

"No."

4

"When?"

"When I'm in the mood."

Slattery frowned.

"Go on now."

"No."

Clenching his hands Slattery leaned grimly across the table and muttered: "Come on, you great English P. Mock me."

But looking directly into Slattery's eyes Lewis smiled, then turned away. "Oh no," Lewis said. "We've gone far enough."

Outside the shutters car hulks blistered; on the slopes gypsy women tipped cartloads of garbage; widows, grandmothers, and children poked and scraped; babies watched from the doors of shacks. Lewis frowned at the dogs, the hobbled donkeys, and the caves.

Beyond the slope vast skeletons of the workers' skyscrapers were deserted in the siesta; Tarmac strips led nowhere; there was a row of unopened shops. Further still the neat bungalows, the sprinklered lawns of the American military. Far away, on a green hill, olive trees, palms, flowers, a walled and guarded estate, a church with a neon cross. Beyond all, a plain of dust and burning mountains, and on the tops of these mountains, in spite of the white sun, snow. "*Viva España*," murmured Lewis.

"Listen, I beg you, you great P., mock me."

But Lewis shook his head so they sat again in silence. The American continued to glare at the Englishman, the *anís* glistening down his neck, a cloud of flies circling above him. Refusing to be disconcerted, stoical in spite of his disappointment, the Englishman whistled Brubeck through his teeth, drummed long fingers on the Formica table top, tapped his sandaled foot on the marble floor.

"Ha, ha, ha. Ha, hardy, ha ha."

"What?"

"You're all faggots, you English. Not that I'd do you any harm."

"Don't be so boring."

"A closet. A closet bloody queen. You see that big blond hooker mincing his way over the trolley lines?"

5

Peering through flies into white light, shading his eyes with his hands, Lewis answered that he did.

"Put on your glasses. Put on your prescriptions."

Lewis did that also.

"Study him."

"Yes."

"What's he doin' out here? That's what I'm askin' myself."

"Yes."

"On a fix. Sort of guy goes to bed with stuffed birds. Not a junkie but nasty. Used to work out of Schwabs. A monster. *Agua caliente*. Keep off his orbit."

"Certainly."

"Wanted to be an actor. Tangled with Sinatra. Dyed his hair. Hardy, ha ha. Keep off his track, he's mean."

"Thank you, thank you."

"Don't drink with him. Keep your face to his kisser. Christ knows what he'd do if he got on your back."

"Has he been on *your* back?"

When Slattery recovered himself he said in an offended tone: "That's not funny, you know."

Laughing, Lewis replied: "Like all piss takers, when it's your turn . . ."

"Aw shut up," said Slattery. "I was telling you the guy's a monster. And don't be disgustin' neither."

A clock struck, a church clock; since the situation between them did not resolve itself in any way Lewis looked out at the slope and Slattery shrugged his shoulders, remarking with indifference: "You have what they call sensitive features."

"My mother used to say that!"

"How dry you are. You're dry, ain't ya?"

"My mother's buried in Madrid. She died on holiday here."

Slattery groaned. "This liquor's touchin' up my prematures. You got a mirror?"

"She's in the British cemetery. We have a cemetery here, you know."

Slattery leaned across the table, knocked a saucer onto the

6

floor with his elbow, punched Lewis in the ribs, and in imitation of Lewis's accent again, announced: "I know you're the sort who carries a mirror."

"That hurt!"

"Buy us another bottle." Slattery punched Lewis a second time.

"You do that again I'll kick you in the balls."

"Haven't got any." Laughing, Slattery threw up his hands like a boxer, laughing he crouched back. "What spirit!" Dropping his hands, Slattery rubbed them round the back of his neck; still laughing he licked his palms, and snorted: "Christ, you're malicious! You know something . . . it's time we had a drink."

Lewis rubbed his side. "What a cruel man you are when you're drunk."

"What do you mean?"

Lewis leaned forward on his rickety chair and stretched out his hands across the table to grip Slattery's arm.

"I was only joking."

Slattery repeated: "What d'you mean . . . cruel and drunk?"

"I'm saying I *didn't* mean it."

Slattery shivered; his mouth opened wide.

Looking intently at Lewis, Slattery disengaged his arm, pushed Lewis's hands off the table, leaned forward on his elbows, and muttered, breathing *anís* and garlic right into Lewis's face: "I don't murder policemen. I don't shoot 'em in the gut and run 'em over in motorcars. Those that do that should be hanged or shot."

Lewis did not move. Again Slattery shivered.

"I don't throw bombs. Castrate Negroes. I don't do burnings."

"No."

"I have my code."

"Yes."

"I don't rape children. I don't rip up a woman with a knife. Misdemeanors, yes . . . felonies, perhaps . . . pravities, not."

"I see," said Lewis.

7

"I am a unique man if you think about it," added Slattery, ironically. "Drunk or sober. I just get frisky sometimes . . . that's all . . . frisky."

"I know," said Lewis. "Indeed I do know that. You are unique."

The two men stared into each other's eyes.

It was Lewis who broke the silence, Lewis who changed his mind and clapped his hands for the boy to come running out of the kitchen and return to the bar, Lewis who asked, "*Más Chinchón, por favor.*"

"*Sí.*"

"*Una botella,*" said Slattery.

"*Una botella?*"

"*Una botella,*" agreed Lewis. "*Una botella y agua minerale. No Chinchón dulce, Chinchón seco. Comprende?*"

"*Sí.*"

Looking back at Slattery, Lewis smiled. "So all right . . . *una botella*. But don't punch me again, and here, comb out your hair, you great American ape."

"What else did your mother teach you? What else did your mother teach ya, you great English faggot? She teach you incest?"

Slattery took the comb and he used it.

"I haven't been to my mother's grave for years," said Lewis. They drank.

"For some time now . . . with my wife I . . ."

"Don't tell me." Seizing the bottle with both hands Slattery began to swig down the rest of the *anís* like soda pop. The flies multiplied. "I don't wanna know."

Rejected, Lewis looked over the glistening head, the enormous slicked-down head, looked up to the plane of brilliant blue sky.

"What you call livin' is dyin' in life," said Slattery. "And what you call dyin' in life is livin'. I got troubles of my own."

Lewis continued to gaze upwards.

"Amazing, this heat; never ceases to amaze ya. Your wife adores it of course . . . adores the heat."

"You don't know what my wife adores; you've never met her."

"I don't intend to."

"I don't intend you should."

"What a tan she's got." Slattery put down the bottle and started to laugh again. "The way that woman can brown herself up. Those thighs of hers. She's got to watch her weight of course. What that woman needs is Guinness."

Slattery tipped the bottle up, threw back his head like a sea lion.

"She is a little on the thin side," said Lewis.

"That sort of doll I detest," said Slattery. "That sort of doll keeps on bein' girlish."

"But you've never seen her," said Lewis. "And as a matter of fact the heat upsets her."

"I don't have to see her," said Slattery. "I know her, don't I?"

Not wishing to continue this line of conversation, realizing that this was no day for intimacy with Patrick Slattery, Arthur Lewis took a thin cigar from the breast pocket of his mohair jacket, snipped off the end and lit it: placing his elbows on the table top, resting his chin on his hands, the cigar now hanging slack from his mouth, puffing and drawing, resuming his gaze above, Lewis began to consider if he could get Slattery back to Madrid without Slattery's taking offense, and before Slattery got any drunker.

Slattery looked at him, tipped up the bottle, grinned.

"Not a cloud. Not a wisp," said Lewis. "I do miss the . . ."

"Rain." Slattery put the bottle back on the table, wiped his mouth and his grey mustache with his yellow sleeve. "I hate nature lovers."

"Will you never go back?"

"Back where?"

"Home."

9

"No."

"Why not?"

"I can't."

"Why not?"

"What a nosy bastard you are. Want to see my passport or somethin'?"

"No, no, of course not. I must apologize for asking."

"Just got into a little trouble. Nothin'. Nothin' at all. Far too much was made of it. Just got a little drunk . . . once or twice . . . havin' a good time. Let's get outta here, I'm bored."

Lewis nodded, called the barman, paid with a note, waited for the change, threw five pesetas onto the saucer.

But Slattery too had waited, and Slattery picked up the five pesetas from the saucer, and put the coin into his pocket.

"I need that," said Slattery. "I'll be needin' that today."

The barman looked up at Slattery, shrugged, went back to the bar.

Lewis too thought it better not to speak.

When they had walked out into the white light Lewis asked: "Would you like me to lend you some money?"

Slattery did not answer. Watching him as he rolled along in front Lewis noticed he showed no physical effects of the *anís*.

"I couldn't lend you a great deal, but I do have an income . . . a small income of course. It would be my pleasure to . . ."

"Help out."

"Yes, help out."

"I don't want your money."

They walked on.

"That's because I've got nothin' against you," said Slattery. "Not yet."

Far away there was an uproar of bells. At the end of the street Slattery stopped, undid his zipper, and urinated against the wall of a house, near two *señoras* sitting on their doorstep. When the women muttered at him he took no notice.

"Wait until I *have* got something against you," said Slattery, "I'll take your money then."

10

They went on.

"You might have found a corner," said Lewis. "That's not nice you know, not kind."

"I should've splashed 'em," said Slattery. "Yes, I'll take your money then!"

The sun burned. On they sweated, Lewis looking resolutely ahead because of the refuse at his feet. Although it was only two o'clock Lewis already had the feeling of another wasted day. Whatever my destination, thought Lewis, it seems to recede when I advance.

Lewis sat sighing, gazing up at swallows, a dwarf polishing his brogues; sipping Campari and soda, sticking a long slender forefinger into his glass, stirring the ice, sucking his finger, spearing sardines and anchovies, biting olives.

Passing down pesetas, Lewis murmured: *"Gracias. Gracias."* Lighting one of his thin cigars, taking out his spectacles, Lewis unfolded a copy of the *Sunday Telegraph* on the table before him, and reread the theater review.

In the dusk the clouds of swallows turned black. On came the green fluorescent; Philip III's horse shone ebony. Out of the restaurants drifted the smell of the lobsters and the omelets; out of the cafés the stink of the oil.

"Wife swapping," Lewis muttered. "Wife swapping in the Surrey belt. Wife swapping in the country cottages. Wife swapping in the wet weekends. Wife swapping in the cottages of the mind."

Lewis took off his glasses, folded up the paper again, slipped the paper into the pocket of his jacket—hung carefully over an empty chair—put his glasses into a black leather case, slid the case into an initialed shirt pocket.

"Wife swapping," he said. "But only when drunk."

From a bar below the arches, from beneath a red awning, detouring to pat the dwarf on the head, Slattery entered the plaza and made his way.

When Lewis saw Slattery he took up his newspaper again.

Massive among the children, the couples, and the tiny sailors,

11

his grey head reaching up to the ebony horse's hoofs, unerringly, as the clocks struck nine, Slattery bore down. The man's a giant, thought Lewis.

"*Beba Coca-Cola deliciosa.*"

Lewis did not look up.

"Put on a wig and I'll show you my mother."

"Yes?"

"May I join ya?"

"What?"

"Sorry about that . . . er . . . that day in the country. Very bad. Very bad of me. And I shouldn't have pissed by those women."

Lewis put down the newspaper, looked up, and smiled. "Oh, that's all right. Sit down and have a drink."

"I'm not drinkin'," said Slattery. "I gave that the heave-ho. Haven't had a drop for a week. Been over there sippin' a Coca-Cola."

"Yes?"

"Not since that fateful day have I imbibed."

Slattery spread himself on an iron chair, took out a cigar, lit it, clapped his hands, ordered mushrooms.

"I've been watchin' ya. Over there I was watchin' ya. Why do you keep readin' that paper?"

"I don't know."

"Won't do you no good. Won this in a raffle." Slattery waved his cigar. "These children shouldn't be up so late."

"Puritan," said Lewis.

Looking at Slattery, Lewis saw that indeed Slattery was sober, saw that the hand that held the cigar trembled, saw a pallor upon the face.

"*Beba Coca-Cola deliciosa.* Awful stuff, kid. Rotgut."

"I know."

"Do ya? Do ya, kid?"

"Oh yes."

They looked at each other steadily. Then Slattery winked. They smiled at each other briefly. Then each turned away to the square. The mushrooms were brought; Slattery ate.

12

Five lamps shone from a pyramid; the Red tourists and their wives went inside.

"I'd give a lot for an Aguila Cerveza."

"Don't."

"What's it to you?"

Easter palms drooped from the tiers and the balconies, boys walked with their hands on girls' shoulders; an old woman came out of a slate roof to scold in her grandchildren below.

"Sore at me?"

"Of course not."

Over the weather-vane crosses, over the attics, over the towers, a different tribe of birds, larger than the swallows, circled in the purple sky, descended, settled, and merged.

"The pawnbroker's sign . . . that scepter in the center . . . those circular decorations . . . those brass balls . . ."

"Yes?"

"Bloody oyga diggas!"

"What?"

"Always oyga-ing and digga-ing."

Other old women came out of the slate roofs and leaned without their aprons.

"Can't see up their skirts. Not in this light. Look at those rain spouts. Behind those shuttered windows what vice? Beneath those fantailed porches what orgies?"

The shrubs were trimmed in the wood-strapped iron boxes; there were television antennas and spires, barometers and clocks.

"Christ," said Slattery, hissing for a waiter, "I must have somethin'. Get me some *calamares. Calamares, por favor.* I must have somethin' or I'll die."

Buzzing out from a café, a fly drew breath, then made for their table.

"I've been readin' about this Strangler."

"What?"

"This Boston Strangler. See that girl with the blue coral plastics stickin' out of her ears."

"They're ceramics."

13

"She's pretty. I once had a great time with two whores in Lisbon. Looked after me like a baby. Couldn't wait to wash my clothes. No rent. Felt bad about it and left them. One guy in Boston laid two thousand women in two years. What about that?"

The *calamares* arrived.

"Yes, I left them. They cried: I cried: we all cried. Such is life."

Lewis waved at the fly, took up his paper, waited to swat: the fly settled on Slattery's nose.

"Interesting perspective," said Slattery, squinting up at the fly, leaving the fly where it was: Lewis put down the newspaper.

"This is like eatin' knickers. I know that's the word you use. I know that, Arthur."

The clack of the high-heeled stilettos on the cobbles diminished; the red-striped taxis went out through the arches.

"Tell me about your wife," said Slattery, leaning forward, wiping his hands on a paper napkin. "Finish that conversation we began so easily."

Lewis frowned.

"It's okay." Slattery sat back in his chair. "I won't gnaw you."

"No."

"Still offended with me?"

"I'm not offended with you."

"Some other time?"

"Yes."

Slattery put out his cigar. "The nights are drawin' in, ain't they?"

"Yes."

"I'm feeding on my own fat . . . which is considerable!"

"You do look slimmer."

Slattery laughed. Slattery went on laughing. "I know you use the word knickers."

"Oh I do," said Lewis. "It's my favorite word."

Red tourists in blazers began to emerge from the restaurants. Taxis re-entered the square. Brown Spaniards got out and went

14

to eat. "The change-over," said Lewis. "Good night. It was nice to see you." Lewis rose, took up his newspapers, and put on his jacket. Lewis shook Slattery's hand, threw down a note upon the table, and went his way through an arch.

A black cloud hovered over the sierra. It had thundered. And yet there was no wind: the red-and-yellow flags hung limp.

Lewis jerked his Alvis through a gap in a traffic jam, revved it onto a building site, got out, closed the roof, locked the doors.

He scuffed his way back over bricks and stones, jumped across drains and ruts, looked down at his shoes and swore.

He went to the corner.

He had parked too soon: he was still in the suburbs.

He wanted to get to a part of the city he knew. He started to run. He ran through fried leaves and brown parched newspapers, through a burned garden and desolate shrubs. He climbed a wall. He passed statues and dead pine trees. He vaulted over an iron railing and got into an alley. He saw the roof of the Plaza Hotel: he knew he had to cross. He leaned against a plane tree while he waited for the policeman to blow his whistle—beside him a uniformed street cleaner with bare dirty feet rested against a cedar. Lewis offered a cigarette. "*Buenas,*" Lewis said. "I'm in a bad mood, *señor. Muy malicioso.*"

The street cleaner nodded his head.

The whistle raged, Lewis left the cleaner and ran; he ran between their flimsy cars, banging them on their roofs with his hand, shouting back abuse at these Simcas and these Séats.

From the steps of the hotel Slattery watched Lewis with his hands in his pockets while Lewis crossed, wondering if Lewis would see him. Slattery did not call out.

When Lewis reached the sidewalk and went right, Slattery did not follow. Slattery watched till Lewis had gone, then went into the Plaza Hotel.

In the bar of the Plaza Hotel Slattery ordered an *anís* and waited on the black leather beneath the chandelier, in his suit, with his hair brushed back, with a silk tie and a wedding ring on

15

his finger, reading page eight of the international *Herald Tribune*
—yesterday's transactions on the New York Stock Exchange.

Slattery was waiting for a lady, an American lady—for Doris,
Mabel, or Caroline—with enough money in his pocket to buy
her a dry martini, enough pesetas to pay for a cab ride.

Going nowhere in particular, having nothing in mind, hungry,
but not wanting to eat, Lewis trailed up side streets under stars,
touching white walls and chopped trees, whistling without joy,
frowning at the tasteless new furniture in the shop windows,
nodding at women with no intent.

He wandered for hours.

A dark purple sky filled with tobacco smoke; the crowd all
orange, yellow, and green.

"A thousand on Barcelona."

"Straight bet?"

Over the velvet grass the Red Cross wheeled the cripples.

"If you have the home team you've gotta give me odds."

"Six to four?"

"A thousand pesetas to my seven hundred."

"All right."

"You have Madrid then," said Slattery, grinning.

They pushed their way on down the aisle—Lewis carrying the
thin cushions to cover their concrete seats.

Onto the velvet ran the maroon and blue: the crowd jeered.

"That's my bunch," said Slattery with pride.

Onto the velvet ran the white: the crowd went mad with joy.

"And that's yours," said Slattery with derision.

They stood and watched while the players limbered up. The
referee blew his whistle. Lewis was about to sit down when he
felt fingers and jumped high.

"Christ Almighty!"

"Got you."

Delighted, Slattery lowered his fingers.

"You're a leaper," laughed Slattery. "You're a Ralph Boston,
you're a Valery Brumel, you're a Beamon."

Glancing around in embarrassment at the grinning Spaniards behind him, Lewis muttered: "Don't ever do that again."

"You'd win the Olympics. Mexico City. Rome. Tokyo. You'd win 'em all."

"Thank you."

"I'd give you a goose and over you'd go."

"Thank you."

"Is that within the rules? Is that what they'd call an outside aid?"

Raising his two fingers again Slattery fired them into the smoke like a pistol. "That's for my President," he said.

The game began.

In the third minute the sandy-haired Barcelona wing centered the ball from the left with no intent, none of his forwards being up to accept: the Real Madrid center-half went to trap the ball and clear it, miskicked the ball, managed to spin the ball backward in a slow arc over his goalkeeper's head: the ball entered the Madrid net.

In horror the crowd was motionless and silent.

As soon as he realized what had happened Slattery sprang to his feet and shouted with enormous joy: "Ha, ha, ha! Ha, hardy, ha ha. *Viva! Viva! Viva Barcelona!*"

Now the Barcelona players began to race about the field, kiss, and jump into each other's arms.

The white center-half buried his head.

Careless of the growing hostility around him, Slattery continued to shout and slap Lewis on the back.

"That'll teach you, you dumb white idiots. Ha, ha, ha! *Viva Barcelona.*"

"That's the worst own goal I've ever seen."

"Ha, ha, ha," shouted Slattery, sitting down at last. "You've got a peg leg for a back. He forgot to tie up his laces."

"Well," said Lewis, "well."

"Ha, ha, ha!"

"You'd better be careful," said Lewis, glancing worriedly around.

"Anybody molests me I molest him first," answered Slattery.

17

Standing up again, turning about, doubling up his fists, Slattery announced cheerfully to the stricken Spaniards around him: "I say anybody molests me I molest him first. *Viva Barcelona.*"

"For Christ's sake sit down," implored Lewis.

The game began again.

"Go on, defense! Go on, defense! Everybody back for ninety minutes."

"If I'd known you were like this," said Lewis, "if I'd known what a rotten sport you were I'd never have brought you."

"One nothin'," shouted Slattery. *"Uno cero.* That'll do it! *Barcelona uno. Madrid cero."*

The game proceeded.

"Pack your goal. Pack your goal, fellas."

And as if hearing precisely Slattery's constant stream of instruction and acting exactly upon it, Barcelona withdrew all forwards and fell back upon an eleven-man defense.

Madrid attacked.

All the white forwards tore upfield, dribbling, weaving, and shooting.

But they couldn't get through.

And the great black Barcelona goalkeeper caught the ball again and again and again.

"Viva Muhammed," shouted Slattery. *"Viva* Muhammed Ali, the Barcelona greatest. Those white fellas is all ponces."

Whenever there was a decision in favor of Barcelona, Slattery rose to his feet and cheered; whenever the referee gave a foul to Madrid, Slattery rose to his feet and derided.

And now disregarding his own forwards, disregarding all, for himself alone, the great black Barcelona goalkeeper began to catch the white ball and kick it in long, slow, huge high kicks right up into the billowing tobacco smoke. This great black goalkeeper would stand watching the ball soar, hands on his hips, wait, then catch the ball again and kick it again.

"What a fella," shouted Slattery. "What an *hombre."*

"He's not attempting to make a game of it!"

"He's an artist," said Slattery with profound respect. "He's inspired. He's like me when I won at the Garden."

18

At the end of the game when Madrid had spent themselves and Barcelona had won, Slattery jumped over the barriers, thundered across the pitch while the forwards were embracing, and kissed the Barcelona goalkeeper upon his forehead.

They entered the smell of the olives, sat down on wooden stools at a wooden table, clapped their hands for wine.

"I shouldn't mix, I suppose."

"Have a swill," said Slattery. "What a win!"

Although it was so late there remained a trio of unattached women.

"You don't have to get up in the mornin', do ya?"

"Never," answered Lewis, sucking his cheeks. "But I don't like to drink too much."

Under the iron lamps, the fans, and the jugs, a waiter came and they ordered.

"I get ill if I do," said Lewis. "I had a couple of Cuba libres before the game."

"Still hopeful, girls?" inquired Slattery.

"No messing about or I'm off."

Slattery rose and bowed to the ladies. "No pissing about, he says, or he's off. I'll buy the drinks."

"Patrick."

"This man," said Slattery, pointing down at his friend, "is a pubic wigmaker. Let me introduce ya. This man can change your lives. Name your colors."

"Oh hell," said Lewis, rising.

"Please," said Slattery. "Let me sing my song to them . . . let me sing my song to the ladies and I'll be replete, I promise you."

"What song?"

"I'm making it up right now."

"Oh very well."

Slattery bowed once more, and to the tune of "Red River Valley" sang gently to the Spanish women:

> "She had avocado pears for her ear muffs
> And she combed up her new pubic wig

19

And she put on her magnetic knickers
And she went for a ride on his pig."

The women clapped: Slattery sat down: not able to be angry, Lewis too sat down.

After a moment Slattery said: "I had the need."

The waiter brought a brown jug of wine; they filled the tiny glasses, drank them up, and filled the glasses again. Quiet coming over them, they stared at the huge, terrible oil painting of a ventriloquist and his puppets.

" 'The Session's Over,' I believe that painting's called."

"I'm sad now," said Slattery. "I'm so old. Give me that thousand you owe me and I'll pay."

"Whatever I feel . . . whatever I have felt," said Lewis, "I have never wanted, never could, never would, never will, take it out on . . . women."

Lewis handed Slattery a thousand pesetas.

"Take what out? Your dick?"

"You know what I mean."

"I don't."

"I'm not talking about anyone else," said Lewis. "I am not offering judgments. I am not talking about you. I am talking about myself."

There was a pause. "Well, I believe you," said Slattery.

"It's just a rule I have."

"You like women, do you?"

"Not any better than anyone else."

"You're a lucky guy, then. Don't push it."

This last remark of Slattery's made Lewis thoughtful. Pouring himself another glass of wine he looked up at the fan in the black iron pot hanging down from the beam, and sucked in his cheeks again. Slattery too chose to be silent.

The iron bars opposite the open door ran all the way to a slum—on the cement grid there were crosses: Slattery began to trace crosses on the table with his forefinger. Slattery hissed: "Is it too late for *tapas?*"

"Pardon?"

20

"*Mucho tarde por tapas?*"

"*Tapas. Sí, señor.*"

Slattery ordered snails in garlic, tomatoes, and hot peppers. Lewis went on thinking.

"How's the wife?"

"What?"

"I said how's the little wife?"

"Away," said Lewis. "Been away for days. Gone south to a wedding. Costa del Sol. Rich friends of ours. Distant relations. I couldn't face it. Retired people. Like myself. But older. Widow and widower. Knew them in India. Your behavior at that game was disgraceful."

"What about getting a couple of whores then?"

"What?"

"Are *you* deaf? I'll pay. I'm the winner."

"Whatever for?" said Lewis. "Didn't you understand what I was talking about? Don't you understand what I feel about women? Don't you understand what I feel about my wife?"

They left the Bar Casona and sat in the Bar Tabanco.

Lewis ordered snails. When Slattery opened his mouth Lewis leaned over with his toothpick and pushed a snail within.

"Thank you."

"And a bit of sausage?"

"No."

"Here."

Not a jacket in the place except Lewis's. An old woman at the cash register. Strings of onions, strings of garlic. Serrano hams cured in the mountain snow.

"Tell me about your romances, now I'm drunk."

"These napkins don't absorb nothin'," answered Slattery, trying to wipe his chin. Pots of flowers hung from the ceiling; there was sawdust on the floor, the walls were tiled with Goya bullfights.

"I had a good lay last night. She told me she was a nymphomaniac. Poor soul. Her eyes filled with tears. You know what I used to do in Manhattan. Uptown and downtown. East Side and West Side. And Boston too. Those years ago."

21

"No."

"Had a tie like those tiles. Wore it often. Yes, I'd go into a bar in a smart hotel. Never the same bar. There's plenty of hotels in America. They're getting to know me at the Plaza. There . . . the Oak Bar, the French Bar, the Ivy Bar, I'd sit myself down by a woman. I'd sit myself down and I'd wait while she ordered . . . watch while she drank . . . watch while she paid. Then I'd put my hand over her change. She'd look at me."

Slattery laughed.

" 'That's mine,' I'd say."

Slattery stopped laughing.

"If she protested, called the barman, or she said somethin', which wasn't often, I'd take my hand off and give it back to her. I'd laugh at her and say I was jokin'. 'Can't you take a joke, it's almost Christmas?' Then I'd buy her a drink and probably lay her. I'd go upstairs if she was old and I'd almost certainly turn off the air conditionin' and I'd lay her."

"What a monster you are."

"Of course, if she didn't protest . . ."

"You'd take the money."

"That's it."

"What were the percentages?"

"Half and half. I always got something."

"There must have been an exception or two."

"Well, I didn't get rich," answered Slattery. "I didn't get rich but I made enough to get by, my friend."

Wading through sawdust they left the Bar Tabanco.

"I didn't like that story," said Lewis.

"I'm what they call a remittance man."

"What's that?"

"Paid to keep out of America."

"Who pays?"

"The President. No. My dad. L.B.J. Slattery. They caught me there."

"Your dad?"

"And my brothers."

"Yes?"

22

"And my sisters' husbands."

"I don't know whether to believe you or not."

"Believe me, boy, believe me."

"Well I find it very disheartening," said Lewis. "I don't know . . . you *can* be so likable."

"It's my smile that gets 'em."

Again Slattery laughed.

"There's more to it than you know," said Slattery. "I seek to disguise the truth. That's the only way I can tell it."

They walked down the narrow street. The black cloud must have blown off the sierra—though the night was hot the air felt clearer. "Sometimes I tell 'em I'm impotent. That's a great comer-on."

"What does your father do?"

"English always ask that. Police chief in Boston. Worked the beat, New York City. One brother's a judge. You're thinking a typical pattern no doubt. Youngest judge in America, my brother."

"I was," said Lewis.

"You're a romantic, that's your trouble."

"Oh shut up," said Lewis. "You've no idea what I am!"

Lewis stopped and stared into a refrigerated window—the window of the Restaurante Rojo. It seemed to Lewis an altar —lamb, veal, pork, steak, chickens, salamis, cheeses, and fish.

"Press your head against this window. There's baby pig, there's oxtails, there's kidneys, there's sweetbreads, and there's brains."

"And blood and flies no doubt."

"Blood and flies and blocks of ice."

Lewis turned. "What I don't understand is why I like you."

Drawn by the flamenco, Lewis entered the Bar Grabieles not caring if Slattery followed. Returning to Cuba libres, Lewis felt a moment of nausea but he swallowed quickly, and the sickness passed.

"Where's mine?" asked Slattery.

They sat in a corner next to a tiled rape.

They drank and Slattery got two more.

"What's that? Rubens?"

23

"Spanish artisan."

"That naked man in the wine cellar: is that his dick?"

"Of course."

"Why do they allow that?"

Looking at him to see if Slattery was joking, Lewis saw that Slattery was not.

"Shouldn't allow such things in a public place. That's what's wrong with this world now, all these love-ins. It was my brother who did most wrong. Yes, it was my sad brother Arnold."

"Let's listen to the singer."

"You can listen to the singer any time. What about my brother Arnold? My brother Arnold, who's dead."

However, Slattery paused, and did not continue, and Lewis was able to listen out the song, sing with the singer, and clap his hands.

"Why don't you get up and dance?"

"I would if there was room."

"What I do is I get my check, I get my pittance and I cash it, I spend it, and for the rest of the month I live off my wits."

"I'm sure they're considerable."

"You're a joker, ain't ya? It's the rest of the month I live for! I came back one night in Boston when I was a fag . . ."

"What?"

"You *are* deaf. I came back one night in Boston when I was a fag, and I had a little talk with Antonio, and finally I hit him over the head . . . with a hammer. He'd become what they call a urinal man. Always hanging around the urinals. It wasn't that he had a lover, no, I'd have forgiven that. It was just those toilets. Those comfort stations. He'd always been that way inclined but never . . . never since I met him. When he became fashionable and they referred to me as his wife . . . people spoke of me as Mrs. Antonio . . . I didn't mind . . . though I couldn't get on with my work. I was glad for him. I loved him but I wasn't loved, you see. He only stayed with me out of loyalty. Out of habit. And because he was mean. He could have gone to a penthouse. They were all after him. He could have gone to a penthouse but I wouldn't stand for it. 'Grow up, Patrick,' he'd say. All that money! 'Grow up, Patrick,' he'd say, laughing . . . wonderful laugh . . . very rich . . . black eyes, Spanish eyes . . . that's why I came to Madrid. So I got the hammer out and I killed him because he'd fallen out of love. After an argument of course. People thought there was another. But that was all lies. That was not so. I was drunk at the time."

"I didn't know you had been . . . were . . . a fag!"

"Oh, I've been everything," said Slattery sadly, "every bloody thing. But that was my brother Arnold, Arthur. Arnold and Antonio; they had an act. It was my sad brother Arnold I was talkin' about. My other brother sentenced him. And my father brought him in."

Slattery frowned; Lewis sucked in his cheeks.

"I've killed," said Lewis.

"Never in the war; not fit to serve . . . ingrowing toenails, they said."

"I stabbed a boy . . . among other things . . . we picked him up . . . was with us for a bit . . . joined us in the mountains. I couldn't take a chance on him. I was the lieutenant so I said I'd do it. In Yugoslavia."

"Does it bother you?"

They went on drinking. They saw clearly: that the wine here was three pesetas a glass; that this was now their bar; that only women were behind this counter; that this place was crowded and the shoeblack had only one leg. Eight pesetas for *anís* and twelve pesetas for Cointreau. The widows selling the lottery tickets; the gutter water springing out in the corners.

"In this place . . . in this place a jukebox is an innovation. Put on a record and play me a couple of bombs. Play me something with napalm in it. Play me somethin' for Franco."

"Shall we move on?"

"Why not?"

"Oh God," said Lewis. "How I love my wife. My wife is enchanting."

The air was calm, this morning, from the city to the lake. Lewis stood for a quarter of an hour, looking back and up.

25

No one at work on the unfinished cathedral—the scaffolding and the red crane, empty. In the mimosa trees a cartload of gypsies.

The workmen in the ditch below stopped digging drains: their babies in their arms, gypsy women advanced to beg. Lewis got on his bicycle, rode away over rock and grass.

When he reached a gap in the palace railings Lewis got off—at his feet a mass of cables and more workmen in a drain. Although the palace stood a hundred yards above him, he stretched out the hand that covered his eyes toward its marble pillars. There was no movement in the rose garden—no gardeners—only leafy arbors, statues, birds, and the long green fountained vista swooping up to grey stone.

Lewis moved on. He pedaled into the Retiro.

He went between cypresses and magnolia trees to the artificial lake; he stared at empty paddleboats. The sun ascended; uniformed keepers came out to pick up litter; he found himself back in that other vast garden, away from that other town, when he was one of the raj.

There were the Victorian statues, there were rhododendrons, fountains, ducks. There were sundials, graveled paths, and lawns as green as Ireland. What of it now? Who was the guardian of that shrine?

A magpie screeched. From that Lewis went to the coming and going: there were corpses in the streets. He thought of a tea party, with Moslem knives outside, and talking with his Hindu friend, drinking his Hindu health, powerless now to protect him, bidding him good night.

"Oh India, land of my fathers," Lewis said. "Should I have stayed?"

Sticking his head through the metal grille Slattery demanded: "Count again."

It was the first of August.

Resignedly the bank clerk adjusted his glasses, wet his finger, and with extreme care, and showing everyone, counted the pile of notes before him a third time.

26

"I can't count it when I'm drunk," said Slattery, "but I figure if you see me watching you do it . . . enough . . . you'll get it right.

"Swindler," said Slattery. "Swindler."

Taking the pile of notes, Slattery rolled out of the bank. He sat on the steps in the sunlight and tried to count the notes himself. When one of the policemen approached him his face lit up with malevolence; stuffing the notes in his hip pocket, he rose and threw up his hands. "Shoot me," he cried.

But beaten down by an unfathomable stare, Slattery turned away, descended the steps, rolled up the street, entered the nearest bar, ordered *anís*.

They knew him there. There by the bank. On the first of the month. Wearing his T-shirt, and his torn trousers. They served him twice, threatened the police, and wiser than before he left.

Outside again he walked across the traffic, holding up his hand like De Gaulle, sat beneath shading trees, and hissed. Again they brought him *anís*. When his rickety chair collapsed beneath him and a half-dozen fat little Spaniards ran to pick him up, he kicked out, bit, and screamed that they were robbers, holding onto his wad of notes with both his massive hands. And presently the friendly Spaniards left him and he rose up, bleeding. He pawed the ground, and goaded them. "Dog," he said. "I'm a mad dog. Take my bone away from me and I get mad and I bite."

Between them they dispersed, persuading each other in whispers to go away and leave him. He continued to rail, calling out: "What learned me to bite? America? You know what happens in this universe to animals that bite?"

He went on abusing the passers-by until he saw the police coming down the street.

Then they all ran.

Hours later he stood in that palace of a white post office, stood in the vast cool hall composing his message. Over and over again he wrote a sentence. Form after form he tore up and stuffed in a basket. He stood there trying to get that message

27

right, trying to compose his masterpiece, trying to put down his epitaph, trying to put down in a single sentence what would be clearly understood in Boston.

On the second of August Slattery stood in the shade in a suit, ants climbing over his shoes, and trembling.

"There is no way to cure me, I am too intelligent."

"I know what you mean."

"What I don't understand is what all these people do. I mean all these people who walk around; what do they do? What are they doin' it for? And why do they go on doin' it?"

"I didn't know about your work," said Lewis. "I'd no idea about that."

"Yeah," said Slattery miserably, "yeah, that part's true. That's the only part that's true. Everythin' else is lies. I've been certified, you know. I have been *in*." Smiling he added: "They let me out as harmless."

"But is your work as bad as you think?"

"That's been confirmed . . ."

"Even by yourself."

"Listen," said Slattery simply. "My work is terrible. I'm tellin' you so you'll know it, without equivocation. I killed myself once but they revived me."

Over the hedge the gardener's cockerels were scratching, beside them leaved branches of pale-green willow trees hung down like sleeves, in the swimming pool tissues of Kleenex floated on patches of sun lotion.

"Well, I've had nothing of a life," said Lewis. "I mean what about me? No children. I don't know who's to blame. We've both had the tests . . . all negative. Perhaps with someone else?"

"I got certificates to prove I'm sane."

"After the war I went back to India. I was there for the breakup, all those murders. Then I went to England again, but I don't really like the place. The money didn't go round and I couldn't fit in. I ran a country club for a while . . . that got me down. That's where I met my wife . . . in Cheltenham. She's much younger than me, as I said. I would like to see your painting for myself."

Slattery did not answer.

"I tried insurance. Very boring. I don't like that way of . . . going on. I inherited something Indian from India . . . no drive. They'll never win a test match. But England's a hopeless place. So crowded. All those awful people. You can't avoid them. And that terrible weather. I suppose I should feel some loyalty to the place. I like the Irish. I might have gone there but then there's all their rain. I am a sun worshiper, you see. I was going to start a restaurant here, you know, curries and all that."

"What a lot of crap," said Slattery. "It's unbelievable!"

"Well, I know," said Lewis. "It's true, though. Do sit down."

Shaking, Slattery slumped into a deck chair.

Sighing, turning onto his naked back, Lewis continued: "What an account of a life. I suppose one lived in the war. Mind you, I do think a good Indian restaurant would do well in Madrid."

Slattery began to laugh. Slattery became convulsed. Tears came to Slattery's eyes. He went to the hedge to vomit.

"You'd bring over your old waiters from Poona? Your old retainers from Delhi?"

Relieved and laughing also, Lewis said: "Of course."

Slattery went on being sick and laughing; Lewis went into the house and fetched out a tray of drinks.

"But Patrick," Lewis said, pouring out iced Fernet Brancas, "we must do something with our lives."

"You can. For me it's too late. Give all your money away. Go to the Congo. Get a divorce!"

"It's all very well to say that."

"What a load of crap."

Disgusted, Slattery picked up the net at the side of the pool, removed the drowning willow leaves and the floating Kleenex. At this sudden violence old hens clucked, lizards ran into the cracks, and the black butterflies flew out of the garden.

"Why have you never asked me here before?"

29

"Because of my wife."

"When's she comin' back?"

"Monday."

"What do you think I'd do to her . . . whip her drawers down?"

"No."

"Might surprise ya. She and I might elope. I only put my suit on because of your wife. I can be nice to the ladies, you know. That's how I live."

In spite of his Panama hat the afternoon sun was too much for him, and leaving the green pool Slattery returned to the shade. "Listen," he said. "I'll be all right with your wife as long as she's no phony."

"Perhaps," said Lewis. "The point is if I did start a restaurant I'd be cooking. At least you *do* something now and again."

Sitting himself on the ivied steps that led to the veranda, pouring himself another iced Fernet Branca, shuddering with distaste, Slattery gazed down at the sun worshiper.

"There's a black beetle on your chest."

Lewis brushed it off.

"And your navel."

Lewis brushed that off too.

"And on your dick."

A pneumatic drill started across the road; siesta had ended. Vespas came clacking around corners; the gardener turned on long black hoses. A mailman arrived with a copy of *Punch*. Courageously Lewis arose and dived through the scum—up and down and around in that tiny pool Lewis swam—Slattery watching with contempt.

The sun got even hotter; it was now impossible to walk barefoot on the swimming-pool tiles.

Lewis hopped onto the grass, brought out his record player, put on Nancy Sinatra.

"Oh Christ," said Slattery.

"*Punch* has really gone off," said Lewis. "It's not funny at all."

At five o'clock a bus creaked by, and a long procession of nuns.

Slattery poured a third Fernet Branca.

"Once we must have had some promise. Or you must have."

"These days!" said Slattery. "There are days I cannot even lift the brush.

"Oh Christ," said Slattery. "Oh Jesus Christ, we are so old."

Ants on the edge of the pool, ants on their feet, ants in the hedges, ants on the steps. Hornets; and a rat going into the drains.

The cracks in the house grew wider, the rusted bolts on the iron doors went molten, the cane roof on the patio sizzled red.

"Christ, it's hot."

And the green leaves kept burning, falling, and turning brown.

"If I don't do somethin' good," said Slattery, at last, "I'll do somethin' awful."

"Oh yes." Lewis looked up from his pool of oil.

"You know how they found that Mary Sullivan? You know how that fella left her?"

"Who?"

"On bed in propped position, buttocks on pillow, back against headboard, head on right shoulder, knees up, eyes closed, breasts and lower extremities exposed, broomstick handle inserted in vagina . . ."

"For Christ's sake," said Lewis, "don't talk about things like that!"

"Well, it's in my mind. It's in my mind, you idiot. That's what I'm *always* talkin' about." Slattery was silent. He looked down at his feet. Then he said: "It's Mother's birthday on Tuesday."

"Now let's get this quite clear," said Lewis grimly, standing up and clenching his fists. "Are you telling me you could *do* something like that?"

"I never have."

"But you fear you could."

Eight-inch lizards hung in the ivy, roses climbed over the bar-

31

becue they never used, dead grey strands fell down the chimneys.

"All these stories I tell ya," said Slattery, "are distractions . . . that's it . . . they're distractions . . ."

"From doing that?"

"What?"

"Hurting . . . being harmful to women. Turning into a maniac."

"No, you idiot . . . from my work."

Throwing up his hands, bewildered but relieved, Lewis sighed and went to a deck chair. "I really cannot believe a word you say."

"You were ready to arrest me."

"I was."

"You would have had a word with the authorities."

"I would."

"Spanish or American?"

"Oh your own, I suppose."

"Ramón, Ramón," called the *sereno*'s wife. On the hour the bus creaked by. Yesterday's papers were dropped at the gate.

"Listen," said Slattery. "I can't paint. I lay women. I'm no good at it. I've got a small income from a rotten father who's a police chief in Boston. What else is there to talk about?"

"Oh I give up," said Lewis.

"So I'm old. So I'm a pathological liar. And I can't hold my drink."

"Thank you. Thank you. Now I see it all," said Lewis.

Moved beyond reason, sure at last that he understood, Lewis was compelled to stretch out his arm and shake Slattery warmly by the hand.

Slattery said: "Yeah, it's Mother's birthday on Tuesday."

2

"Is that you?"

"Yes."

"Get over here. I need a plumber."

"What?"

"Get over here, I need ya. Bring your tools."

"But . . ."

"Nine-eight-nine Generalísimo, Apartment Twenty-seven F."

Putting down the phone, not knowing how Slattery had got his number, and not having seen him since that summer, Lewis hesitated in his hall. The telephone rang again.

"Don't loiter. Bring your tools."

"I think, dear, if we're going skiing, I'll check the Alvis. No antifreeze . . . never thought it necessary. Thaw it out gently with the oil heater and go down to the garage. Mustn't crack the radiator."

Kissing her tenderly, Lewis left.

Backing onto snow chains Lewis fastened them, reversed out of the garage, up the driveway, and onto the street. The snow came in through the roof and fell on his cuff. He drove past the university, taking the long way round. In his pocket he had wrenches and a hammer—in the bag beside him a flashlight and other tools. He drove very carefully over the trolley lines and around the frozen fountains. When he got to the main road, thinking of his tires, he stopped and took the snow chains off.

Answering the door himself, grey, pale, massive, ravaged, but handsome as before, asking, "Got your tools?," Slattery wel-

33

comed Lewis into his hall. "You ain't changed . . . give me your coat."

"Is it warm enough?"

"Sure, central heating."

Seeing that Lewis was surprised at this luxury, surprised at the size of his hall, Slattery murmured: "It's my father, L.B.J. Slattery, who pays for the joint. Take yourself into my drawin' room, I'll make you coffee. The tools can look out for themselves."

Laying the tools under a table in the hall Lewis went into the living room and Slattery down the long corridor.

Because of the snow swirling and beating against the balcony windows Lewis did not at first notice a boy lying on the red plush sofa, under a Mexican blanket. He went to the windows, looked out, putting his hands onto the long low radiators. It was quiet up here; no noise could be heard from below. Lewis stood watching the snow falling on the water towers, the football field, the circus, and the merry-go-rounds.

Entering the room with a tray, Slattery put it down on a radiator.

"Brandy in it?"

"A little."

Reaching for a bottle of Carlos Primero from a sideboard with a marble top, Slattery remarked: "That corpse you're lookin' at . . . take no notice."

"Who is he?"

"Just nobody."

Swallowing, feeling the brandy go down, and almost immediately settle him, Lewis kept gazing at the boy. "He seems to be sleeping so heavily."

"Yeah."

"Is he ill?"

"Last night. Gave himself a fix. He's a friend of mine. It's warm up here. Hides from people up here. Yeah, he's a friend of mine. That's why I let him come up."

Draining his cup, Lewis passed it back for more coffee and brandy.

34

"Do *you* give him the stuff?"

"What?"

"You know what I mean. Are you a dope peddler? A pusher?"

"Are you asking for a kick in the ass?"

"Tell me the truth."

"Of course I'm not," said Slattery, totally offended. "Such was never my line."

"Do you take it yourself?"

"Sometimes took pot. The rest, no." Slattery glanced at the bottle of brandy with longing but did not touch it. Lewis noticed for the first time that Slattery's left hand was swollen. "There was a time I'd give myself a squirt but I kicked it."

"What do you want my tools for?"

"So he looks like the young fella you done . . . the young fella you stabbed in the mountain. I don't want your tools for a coffin. You got a wrench?"

"Yes."

"I tell you he's sleepin'. The rats are returned to their holes. No, it's no coffin. That's not what I want your tools for."

"What'll you do with him when he wakes?"

"Push him out in the snow. I ain't his mother. I don't want women up here. He still has women. Girls and suchlike. I never lay women up *here*. This is *my* place. Did I tell ya I might be gettin' married?"

"No."

"Yeah, I might do that. I'd bring a wife up here."

"Well, that's very good news."

"Is it?" Slattery glanced searchingly at Lewis, then looked over at the boy. "I'll give him a few pesetas, I guess. *That's* why I need your tools. I'd bring a wife up here if I loved her."

Slattery rose, went to the boy, turned up his eyelids, came back. Lewis didn't know whether to inquire further about the marriage, or try to find out exactly what Slattery meant about the tools.

"He ain't interested in sex; the girls don't know that. He don't tell 'em that. You don't lay when you take that stuff." Slattery paused. When he looked like this, Lewis had a feeling of being left out. "No, the boy can't lay and he won't tell 'em. And they hang around hopin' but the porters are all bribed. He'll never kick it, you see, Arthur. Not this boy. Never. He can't stand the boredom. Twenty-two. Can't grow a beard. It'd be just as well if you looked for your old knife, your old piece of military equipment, went out there on the balcony, took the rust off in the snow, came back in here, and cut his throat."

Lewis had nothing to say to that: he had another swallow of the brandy, and, his mind going back to the tools, he asked: "What about my spanners?"

"Spanners?"

"My tools."

"Come from the same town, you see, Boston. I know his elder brother. Small world."

Lewis repeated: "What do you want these tools for?"

"Finish that brandy, will ya, it's driving me nuts havin' to look at it. His brother's a lawyer."

Lewis took the brandy, tipped it up, took a long drink, then went to the sideboard and put it in a drawer.

"That's no good," said Slattery. "I can smell it there."

Lewis took the bottle back out of the drawer, took off the cork again, drank the third of the bottle that remained.

"I must call my wife."

"Do you think I got a phone up here?"

"Oh!"

"I hate the phone."

"Ah."

"D'you think I want them to call me long distance?"

"All right . . . later."

"I always call 'em collect."

"Yes."

"Drugs provide the alternative . . . drink don't do that. The alternative to boredom and to pain. And havin' no talent. Look at that!"

Pointing, rising, pulling Lewis with him, Slattery took Lewis to the window.

36

Like a retreating army, the swirling blizzard was falling back
from Madrid to the plateau, leaving behind its dead: dogs on the
garbage dumps, birds in the telegraph wires, sheep in the fields.
On the high roads abandoned trucks, on the plain abandoned
tractors and carts. Beyond the grey pylons, behind the pueblos
in the foothills, the mountains themselves began to appear; and
the mist, the darkness, the wind, and the snowflakes rolled back
onto the slopes and the pine forests, and up and over the mountain tops, so that a glow of yellow, like dawn, appeared on high.
For a minute or two, above the peaks, above the yellow glow,
huge clouds of mist, sleet, rain, and darkness spun like whirl-
pools to the north of the Guadarrama, onto Segovia, Sepúlveda,
and La Granja. But here, the sun bursting down through the
skies turned them into a brilliant blue and struck the whole vast
white expanse of mountain and plain with such a blaze of light
that the two men raised their hands to their eyes and covered
them because their eyes were dazzled.

"Jesus Christ," said Slattery. "Magic."

Peering through their fingers, accustoming themselves to the
radiance, they watched a last few deserted snowflakes flutter
down from above, gleaming and melting as they came, and van-
ishing on the balcony rail only a yard or two beyond.

Opening the balcony windows Slattery went outside, picked
up snow with both hands, rubbed it all over his face, the top of
his head, and the back of his neck, and stuffing it into his mouth
began to chew and swallow. Lewis too went outside but he was
content to breathe deep and sigh.

When they returned, shut the windows, and lowered a blind,
Slattery said: "I've been thinkin' of takin' a dive from there."

"From your balcony?"

"Yes."

"Are you serious?"

"If I did I'd go down with a blanket. That blanket and my
telegram."

"Telegram?"

Looking at Lewis, Slattery winked sardonically, added:

37

"Blanket to cover the body of course. Now these tools . . . I want you to open a pipe."

"A pipe?"

"I got somethin' in a toilet pipe I want you to get out."

"Here?"

"Yeah."

"You mean it's frozen up."

"No, it's blocked."

"What with?"

Slattery began to laugh.

When he had finished, Lewis asked determinedly: "With drugs?"

"Naw, dollars."

"Dollars?"

"Dollars." Leaning forward, smiling, Slattery was about to continue when the boy on the sofa cried out and turned over onto his face. Both men looked, and listened, but after a moment the boy was quiet, the body relaxed, and once more the boy slept: regaining his ironic smile, speaking slowly in a humorous self-deprecating tone, Slattery began again: "Yes, greenbacks up my pipe. Goya was a revolutionary if not in act . . . in art. It was after his deafness his art took character: I should blow my eardrums out! Goya was a revolutionary but I am a conventional. How can it be that I know so much of that man and share so little? Can't hold a match to his shadow, let alone a candle. Yet I know I'm a better lay. I meant to tell you I was never one for Arabia. I do not like that place. *There* it's *they* who want to do all the layin'. It ain't even fifty-fifty. When they get to manhood they take their revenge, seize you from behind and lay you like a dog. I am speaking of the tourists, of course, I am speaking of being a tourist in Arabia."

"Might we get to the point?"

"Am I borin' ya?"

"Yes you are."

"You see, Arthur . . ." Slattery grinned maliciously, and pointed a finger at Lewis, as if in accusation. "Those Arabs do

38

it with no finesse and I know it is finesse you require in such matters."

Looking at his watch Lewis inquired patiently: "Do you really want me to do something for you with my tools and if so, what?"

"Now I've got ya," said Slattery, "I'm keepin' ya. Goya was a revolutionary, I am a conventional. For conventionals everythin's out but alcohol. No other aberrations permitted." Seizing Lewis's left wrist, twisting it to his convenience, Slattery read the time from Lewis's watch, went to the sideboard, pulled out an unopened bottle of Carlos Primero, uncorked it, and drank. "It's okay now; it's after lunch."

"I'll be going." Lewis rose.

"Sit down, for Christ's sake. Have a drink. I've not even begun. You've opened no pipe. Sometimes I despair of you. Will I let you out in the world and leave me? No, it's safer in here. I need you."

Lewis saw that there was in that face, in those eyes, some need, and having seen it, not being able to deny it, he took the bottle, raised it to his lips, and sat down where he had before. "Unfortunately I am conventionally deranged. You can switch me off and on like a bulb. Another two years of this stuff—" Slattery held up the bottle to the blaze coming in through the slats in the blinds—"and in spite of my magnificent constitution a half a glass of sherry'll be doin' it. Now I may push that state because it's cheaper, I may kick it, or I may kick life. That I have been gettin' nearer to, of late, on my balcony. I think death comes with age. Yes, I am an untalented conventional. I know that, *that* has been one of my many troubles. Goya began late . . . his beginnings were no augury. No one could have foretold."

"Don't give up hope," said Lewis.

"I'm descended from Puritans." Slattery took the bottle from Lewis, and drank again, looking mournfully at Lewis while he did so. "My mother's old, now. She's old." Slattery sighed. "How can a man like me paint so bad?"

39

"I don't know that you do. Who says that you do? I'm no judge, of course."

"Your opinions would be irrelevant."

"My opinions would not be irrelevant."

Considering Lewis, Slattery inclined his head. "Sometime, then, sometime."

"Why not now?"

"Oh not now," said Slattery. "Not *now!*"

"Why not now?"

"Because I couldn't stand it!"

Slattery said this last sentence so loudly that Lewis looked over to the boy to see if the noise had woken him up: the boy slept as before.

"How far can a man go . . . before . . . he's obliterated?"

Lewis had the feeling that though the afternoon was going to be interminable, it was necessary for him to endure it. His thoughts included his wife and he began to consider what best to tell her when the moment came for him to telephone.

"I have painted in shacks where there was so little room my ass was out of the door in the middle of winter. I couldn't block the window because of the light. Whatever you do, wherever you go, whoever you lay, that family of yours rubs off on ya! Heroin is habit formin'. Marijuana turns me against myself, but to live . . . to live with the naked mind . . . takes courage."

Lewis's thoughts returning to his own eternal problem, he did not hear what Slattery was saying.

"I shall find myself lost in the dark with nothin' to play with. Life's a train. Yeah. Life's a train rollin' to death, and everythin' you do, you do on the train. Except for opium! Yeah, opium's the only thing different from life and death. Maybe I should get a cat but I never liked cats. Beware of habit. Even good ones. Look at my broken hands . . . they're covered with paint, but they're not the hands of a master. My father caught me once pissin' in the sink. He was brutal. My father pisses ice water."

Lewis was distracted from his thoughts and his own dilemma by the realization that Slattery had banged him on the knee.

40

"Listen, for Christ's sake. Goya was bullnecked. I am bull-necked, there the resemblance ends. Those grey portraits, those grey-green portraits, those first essays are odd. They are odd. Did you ever see such grey-green people . . . like flat dolls? I am comin' at it from all sides because the frontal attack is obsolete. Yes, I have been a user, I have wasted like the boy there, but *I* kicked it. I have been like my son there . . . but no more for me . . . the cop-out."

"Your son?" Lewis sat up straight.

"Just jokin'," said Slattery, laughing. "Got to keep your attention. To be a user is to let the air out of your soul. I use that word because of my mother. It's great when the air's issuin' forth, it's great when you're bleedin' . . . but you can't work. You can't work, and you don't work. My mother has a soul!"

Rising from his chair Slattery went over to the sleeping boy, kissed him gently on the forehead, and returned.

"Is he your son?" demanded Lewis.

"That's a long mumble. A long acid mumble. And it's only yourself that hears it. No, I've been there except that I always washed my dick. My mother taught me that. Me and two females, that's different, but not six filths in a bed! No, I don't go for that, and I always wash my dick before and after." Turning in his chair, looking back at the boy, inviting Lewis to do the same with a jerk of his head, Slattery continued: "To be a user is also to lay the veins open, not only to cops but also to substi-tuters, cheats, and rats. Your fixer can poison you with aspirin if he has the mind. Though we are all in others' hands, Arthur, to be in others' hands is bad. Turn him violet; and you can be laughin' while one of the acquaintances dumps him in the parkin' lot."

"But do you mean this boy's dying? Is he your son and is he dying?"

"Listen to me. I always listen to you. Disease is on the increase."

"Have we got to take this boy out and leave him on a parking lot?"

"Relax. You've had experience. You've murdered. He ain't

41

turning blue, for Christ's sake. I am speaking of myself. I am not speakin' for others, or him, or that other kid you killed in the mountains."

Lighting himself a cigar, Lewis said: "But that was when I was young. I'm not young now. I am not young. I am old."

"Ah."

There followed a long pause.

"Art is the only way."

"What?"

"There's bodies on every corner. Blood on every road. How do you paint it?"

Clenching his fist, shaking it at Lewis, who found himself so irritated at that moment that he would have welcomed a blow from Slattery and returned it with interest, Slattery continued: "The present situation defies description. I can't do it for ya, I can't begin. Blood melts in my mouth: I can't distill it. Me! I paint like a critic. Believe me. You are old but my mother is older!"

Lewis rose.

"Where are you goin' now?"

"Home!"

"Sit down."

"But my wife . . ."

"Fuck your wife."

Lewis frowned.

"I know it is in that region *your* dilemma lies."

"Don't talk about my wife like that."

Slattery smiled—Slattery smiled a child's smile, looked up at Lewis, and asked forgiveness.

"No more of this," said Slattery. "Let's go into the toilet. First you go downstairs and make a call to the little wife, then come back up here and we'll open my pipe. Let's have some action."

Slattery sat on the edge of the bath with the brandy bottle in his hand, gazing at the toilet pipe.

42

"Sh," said Slattery, holding two fingers to his lips. "This Spanish plumbin' carries."

"Come on," said Lewis, "I promised to be home for tea."

"What else did ya promise?"

"Nothing. I told her there was trouble with the car."

"All right," said Slattery. "Look."

Following the direction of Slattery's somber stare, Lewis too considered the toilet cistern and the toilet pipe.

"In there . . . three months' allowance . . . birthday . . . Christmas bonuses. Eighteen hundred dollars. Most I ever had."

Out of his trouser pocket Slattery pulled a wad of sodden notes, laid them on the bath mat, took the bath mat to the radiator, placed mat and notes upon it.

"These I recovered."

"From where?"

"From the top."

Lewis looked at the cistern.

"How much?"

"Two hundred."

"So there's sixteen hundred inside."

"But that I spent last night. Spent or gave away. Or was stolen from . . . or lost."

"How much was that?"

"Maybe fifty. I only went out the second time with fifty."

"The second time?"

"I came in here and put 'em in the cistern for safety. I forgot that till a kid came in here . . . came in here this morning. Wouldn't flush. Kept tryin'."

"So they're blocking the pipe?"

"Yeah."

"None came through when he pulled the chain?"

"No."

"How did you flush it?"

"With a bucket from the bath. There were two notes come through . . . but they were only fives . . . so I let 'em go."

"Ah."

43

"What's a couple of fives?"

"What indeed!"

"And I pissed in the night. Don't know what went down then. Wasn't lookin'."

"Hmm."

"Wish to Christ I'd used the sink."

A profound gloom settled over Lewis.

"Do somethin'," said Slattery, irritated. "It's not your loss."

"You said you hid them there for safety," Lewis queried, still trying to piece together the story, and to collect his own thoughts. "You put your dollars in the cistern?"

"When I get drunk I have a persecution complex."

"Yes."

"I figured they was gonna rob me or somethin'."

"Oh."

"I figured they did rob me. I hit one of 'em over the head with a bottle."

"A Spaniard?"

"Naw, an American."

"Well, thank God for that."

"Yeah, I seen him."

"How is he?"

"I apologized."

"But how is he?"

"He ain't too good. He ain't too bad."

"So you mean," said Lewis slowly, and after a pause, "you came up here, drunk, and hid your money in the cistern for safety, and then went out and found the money wasn't in your pocket, and forgot you'd put it in the cistern, and thought one of your friends had stolen it, and you hit him on the head with a bottle?"

"Somethin' like that."

"Somethin' like that?"

"Yeah. Well, exactly like that!" said Slattery.

Slattery dropped his eyes and looked at the floor; Lewis looked back at the toilet pipe.

"One of the kids, the one who came for the crap, did take a

44

bill, a twenty-dollar bill, and I chased after him and he ran away laughin' and I couldn't catch him . . . though I used to be a runner . . . I used to be a runner, did you know that?"

Hearing the note of aggrievement Lewis looked back from the pipe.

"I ran at the Garden, did you know that?"

"No."

"Was one of the first Americans to break four ten. Mind you, the kid ran up an alley. He ran up an alley and I lost him."

"And this morning he brought it back."

"Yes," answered Slattery, frowning, "come round here and brought it back."

"And told you he'd only taken it so you wouldn't spend it, told you that, I suppose."

"Somethin' like that," agreed Slattery, "yeah, somethin' like that."

"And it was only when he came in here and couldn't flush your toilet you . . ."

"Aw, shut up," said Slattery. "For Christ's sake open the bloody pipe. That Jim Ryun's gonna break three fifty."

Lewis stood up and went to the toilet pipe. He studied it. He saw that behind the cistern, at the top, the pipe that carried the down-flushing water disappeared into the bathroom wall before it reappeared to enter the toilet bowl several feet below.

"Don't tell me," said Slattery.

Standing on the toilet seat, removing the cistern lid, laying it on the floor, Lewis put on his glasses and remounted.

"Hand me the flashlight," said Lewis.

Slattery did so, and Lewis scanned the waters. "Nothing in here," Lewis said.

"I know that!"

Feeling into the waters with his long slender fingers Lewis found that the notes must have slid under a large cylinder before entering the pipe itself, but the gap between the cylinder edge and the bottom of the cistern was not large enough for him to get his fingers properly underneath. Moreover, the edge of this gap was slimy and unpleasant: he took his fingers out.

45

"Have you got a colander?"

"What?"

"A sieve."

"I've got a French fries basket."

"Well, get it," said Lewis. "Whatever we do we have to make sure no more money goes down the emptying pipe."

"Jesus, you're right," said Slattery. He hurried out of the bathroom and came back with a metal basket.

"Good," said Lewis. Nodding his head, Lewis took the basket, bent its handle inside, wedged it down into the toilet bowl so that it covered the exit pipe, then went to the washbasin.

"Disinfectant, please."

Slattery handed Lewis a bottle of Lysol. Lewis poured it over his hands.

"But none into the bowl," said Slattery. "Don't want it rottin' no greenbacks. That's powerful stuff, that Lysol."

Going to the toilet chain, Lewis took the end of it, nodded purposefully to Slattery so that Slattery came over beside him to look into the bowl, and gave the chain a fierce tug: there was a clank, a dull roar, and a hiss: then the waters above them subsided; nothing at all came down into the toilet bowl. They waited. Nothing at all.

"I told you," said Slattery. "I told ya. The bloody thing's stopped up."

In the silence that followed, Slattery took another drink from the bottle of brandy, wiped the neck with his hand, held the bottle out to Lewis; but Lewis demurred.

"Quos vult perdere dementat."

"What?"

"He drives mad those he wishes to destroy. I went to high school."

"We have to turn off the water so that when we dismantle the pipe it won't come pouring down."

"You mean out of the inlet pipe?"

"Yes."

"But it won't do that if we don't pull the chain."

46

"It might if we start interfering with the cylinder. And anyway—" Lewis paused—"it leaves us so vulnerable."

"No!"

"No?"

"I can't go down to those *porteros*. They tell the management . . . I get thrown out. They're looking for that. Looking for a complaint."

"There've been previous complaints?"

"What do *you* think?"

"Then let's stop it up with corks and tissues."

"Yeah, but we can't turn the water off without those *porteros*," said Slattery sadly. "And anyway I want no one to know about this but yourself."

Lewis sat down for a moment on the edge of the bath. Touched, he nodded his head in acknowledgment.

"So you didn't tell the boy, then; the one who came in here!"

"I told no one but yourself," said Slattery. "Let's have a break."

"No, I'm not going out drinking."

"I don't mean that . . ." Slattery paused, took another drink from the bottle, looked over the top of it at Lewis and muttered: "Come on, I'm gonna show you my work." Without another word Slattery rose and left the bathroom, not looking back to see if Lewis followed.

At the end of the long corridor Slattery stopped, fumbled in his pocket, produced a key, unlocked the door in front of him. Over the door there was a notice: *No drink allowed in here!* Slattery kicked the door open, reached back, grasped Lewis by the arm, and pulled Lewis into the room past him. Advancing onto the threshold behind Lewis, Slattery waved a hand, then giving Lewis a glance that seemed to Lewis to contain both pride and shame, muttered something that Lewis could not hear, and withdrew, shutting the door as he did so. Lewis stood: for a moment he had the curious impression that Slattery was about to lock him in. Lewis stood still while Slattery stumbled away down the bare wooden corridor; then he turned and looked about him.

47

The room was stacked with canvases from top to bottom. These canvases stood in roughly constructed partitions and shelves both in the center and at the sides. At a window two easels, with paintings upon them—there was nothing else but palettes, brushes, paint, shadows, sunlight, and dust. Feeling himself hemmed in by the number and size of these stacked partitions and shelves, feeling also that from somewhere in these crowded walls, or from the ceiling above, Slattery was still gazing at him, not knowing what to look at first, Lewis walked down the passage in front of him toward the light, but when he reached the paintings on the easels, unable to consider them before he had a cigar, he eased past them, took out a cigar, lit it, and stood with his back to the mausoleum, peering out and down at the melting snow, the cars, and the people on the silent avenue. Lewis went on standing at the window—ash formed on the edge of his cigar. Not thinking it right to drop ash on this floor, he raised his hand to open the window, and it was only then that he noticed that he could not do this, and realized why the room was so silent: Slattery had fixed a sheet of glass across the inside of the window making the window double-glazed. Drawing deep on the thin cigar, Lewis shook the ash into the cuff of his left trouser leg, tiptoed back from the gleaming snow and the sunlight, and stood between the two easels, cleaning his glasses with his handkerchief, straightening his tie, tightening the knot, and pulling down his jacket—not with vanity, but for Slattery's sake, as a mark of respect—and at last he put on his glasses and looked.

Both paintings were glued to pieces of cardboard on thin plywood in the manner of the old painters of Siena. Both were oils.

The painting on his left was of a mother and child floating on a cloud in the shape of a bed—an orange cloud in an orange sky. Orange clouds and orange mists. The child was nursing the mother. The bed swam so perceptibly it seemed to Lewis that at any moment it might vanish.

After a moment Lewis found it beautiful.

48

"Thank God," Lewis muttered.

Shaking off the ash into his cuff again, listening for footsteps —hearing none—Lewis went slowly down the passage to the far corner of the room, looking at other paintings of other times.

It was their gentleness that astonished him. And the softness of their colors.

Here the women were in threes. Trios of mothers with chubby formless hands plucking at their breasts—which were cellos, string basses, and guitars—gazing out of their canvases with sad, averted, hooded eyes, playing tunes for their children.

Lewis put out his cigar on the sole of his shoe, put the butt into his jacket pocket.

Here was canvas after canvas painted over and over and over; layer upon layer of female nudes—young girls, young wives, mothers, grandmothers, matriarchs, and little children.

An old woman sat contemplating water and trees. Both sun and moon shone in the sky. Below the woman a walled city with a Moorish church. Around the city a brown plain with green spring corn and red summer poppies. In the distance, mountains.

Behind the old woman, on the summit of a hill, other old women were digging a grave for a child.

Telling himself that he knew nothing of painters or painting, telling himself that he knew nothing of art, Lewis was certain he could live with these works.

Slattery was not by the toilet pipe, not in the kitchen. Slattery sat in a chair before the balcony windows, gazing across the white plain at the white mountains. "Do not speak," Slattery said. "Say nothin'."

Crossing the room, Lewis drew up a chair and sat down beside Slattery to look out also at the sun and the melting snow: starving though he was, thirsty though he was, Lewis did not glance at his watch, or stretch out his hand for the bottle on Slattery's knee. Nor did it occur to him to go and work on the toilet pipe. Lewis sat there with Slattery, content to watch the wind blow the loose snow from the rooftops, watch it scudding

49

along the crusted building sites, the fields and the plain, watch it lifting and whirling away in eddies and in clouds.

"Viva. Viva la muerte!" Looking at Lewis, and raising his bottle. "You say nothin' of my work."

"You told me not to speak."

"You say nothin' of my technique . . . nothin' of how I use paint . . . nothin' of how I put it on."

"I'm not qualified to talk of technique. I can only say what I feel about . . ."

"Arthur," said Slattery. "Keep quiet, will ya."

The shadow of the sun began to glide across the plain toward them. A moon rose over Barajas. Flapping with upturned wings and skidding like gulls in the sea, a flight of crows landed on the football field, took off at once to the garbage slopes by the Burgos road. The sun grew paler. The wind grew colder. The snow stopped melting. The drops on the balcony froze. In the distance donkeys brayed.

Clocks struck. There was a confused bleating. Old men in blankets drove sheep from a side street, crossed the trolley lines, crossed the main road, crackled the thin white ice at the traffic circle. The dogs paused and rolled in the clean snow.

Stars began to slide toward them with the moon and the sun. They could see the whole circle of the sky slowly turning upward. They could feel their apartment block gently tipping over. Stars fell forward into their room.

"I love your paintings. You know that. They're beautiful."

"Beautiful?"

"Yes."

"A Victorian word."

Rising, glancing down at Lewis, Slattery went to the sleeping boy.

He bent his head.

"Not dead, then," Slattery said.

"He's been sleeping for hours."

"Good luck to him."

"Do you only paint women?"

50

"Women and children."

Nodding to Lewis, Slattery left the room.

After a moment Lewis heard the front door bang.

Lewis too went over to the sleeping boy.

Lewis saw that Slattery had tucked a ten-dollar bill into the waistline of the boy's jeans.

Coming out of the bathroom, Lewis re-entered the living room to get the cork from the empty brandy bottle. The boy slept as before. Lewis had got the cork, was leaving the room, when he hesitated, went over to the boy, and stuck a thousand-peseta note into the waistline of the boy's trousers beside Slattery's ten-dollar bill. Sighing, Lewis returned to the bathroom, wrapped toilet paper round the cork, took off his shoes, stood on the toilet seat and after two or three adjustments managed to wedge cork and paper into the intake pipe. Lewis got down off the seat, left the bathroom, went to Slattery's kitchen—which he noticed with surprise was extremely clean and tidy, and well-stocked with spices and herbs—found a tin mug and a small bucket, returned to the bathroom, got onto the toilet seat, and began to bail out the water into the bucket, patiently and slowly, being extremely careful not to spill any of the water onto the wall or the floor. When he had done as much as he could with the mug he got down off the seat, emptied the bucket into the bath, left the bucket where it was, returned to the kitchen, found sponges and rags under the sink, went back to the bathroom, took up the bucket again, climbed onto the seat again, and proceeded to mop up the remaining water and squeeze it into the bucket.

Emptying the bucket into the bath a second time, Lewis went again to the kitchen. Searching the cupboards, he found at last what he wanted, took a pile of old newspapers back to the bathroom and spread them carefully, several layers thick, on the floor around the toilet bowl. Then he took up his wrench, stood on the seat again, adjusted the wrench, and began to undo the nut at the top of the pipe underneath the cistern.

51

Coatless in the freezing night, fingers clenched, thumbs pushed into his ears, elbows resting on the stone parapet of the *puente,* Slattery leaned out like a gargoyle and stared down into the shadows, smiling.

"Aún aprendo."

Trains whistled in the Estación del Norte.

A full white moon shone down. The rooftops gleamed. The statues were etched in ink. His breath steamed.

"Aún aprendo."

The night grew colder but he took no notice. The parapet creaked with frost.

"Aún aprendo." He looked up at the sky, still smiling, his thumbs still in his ears.

Stars flared, vanished, and flared again.

The parapet was now as white as paper and his elbows were frozen to it.

When he took out the bottle from his jacket, his sleeves crackled.

He drank, put back the bottle.

The bells tolled: he left the bridge. The bells tolled all the way to the church—the church of San Antonio de la Florida.

There were lights within and he entered.

There were burning candles, priests, and black cleaners, but they took no notice of him.

He dipped a finger into his bottle, crossed himself with brandy on his forehead.

Then he went to the cupola to pay his respects to the remains brought down from Bordeaux, buried beneath. He got down on his knees, closed his eyes, bowed his head.

Raising the bottle again, he tipped back his head, he drank. "Francisco," he said, "I love you."

He got up from his knees, left the cupola, went to an aisle and lay down on his back there to gaze up at the frescoes on the ceiling, at the court ladies and the angels.

After a quarter of an hour he returned to the cupola, lay down there with his bottle, smiling peacefully up at St. Anthony raising the dead.

Slattery was still smiling when he re-entered the bathroom, where Lewis had unscrewed both top and bottom of the pipe, and now sat staring at this pipe with its open ends protruding, and its remainder still hidden in the wall.

"Ah, you're back."

"I am. I'm back. That's what I am. I'm back."

"Now what do we do? Pull this pipe out of the wall?"

"What?"

Lewis rose from the edge of the bath and went toward the pipe. "I've drained the bottom of it."

"What?"

"I've drained the bottom of it. I've thrown that water away, and I've siphoned the top of it . . ."

"What?"

"I siphoned the top of it with this rubber tube." Lewis bent down and showed Slattery some thin rubber tubing. "I went down and bought this and siphoned out the water from the top into your toilet but no money's come out yet. All the money must be stuck together and jammed."

"The painter's friend," said Slattery, taking a drink from his bottle and sitting down with his back to the wall, on the floor by the doorway, "said to the painter, 'I like your paintings, I like your compositions, I like your sense of balance, I like your colors . . . they belong where they are . . . everything is so pleasing. Will you tell me how did you learn these abilities?' "

"Oh yes," said Lewis. "Oh yes, that's well put, I did feel that."

"Did ya?"

"Oh yes."

"Francisco," said Slattery, "lived in the Quinta del Sordo, deaf-man's villa, high over the Manzanares, beyond the Puenta de Segovia. Wife dead. Friends in exile. Very lonely. *Visiones fantásticas*. Pathos, mystery, and terror intermingled. *Aún aprendo,* you see . . . ever-learning."

53

"Yes," said Lewis, glancing at him. "Remarkable. Yes, I've seen them often. Now we could either get a wire and poke it through, though that might destroy or damage some of the notes as they're wet . . . even dollars . . . or just wait for them to dry. Perhaps they would flutter out of their own accord, but it depends on how quickly you need the money and how quickly you want to use your toilet again, and anyway there is of course a bend in the pipe, so I don't . . ."

"Flutter out of their own accord, you say?"

"Possibly."

"Like leaves?"

"Perhaps!"

"Depending on how soon I want to crap?"

"Yes."

"Or we put a ferret down? Or a rat? Hood up a rat and put it down. Put a rat in the top end . . . block it . . . set a trap with cheese at the bottom."

"No, no."

"We could poison the rat before we put it in."

"I think we should pull the pipe out of the wall, and heat it on one of your radiators."

"What?"

"If we dry it, we might even be able to blow it out."

Shrieking with laughter, spilling brandy onto his trousers, sitting up straight, Slattery cried: "You think we can blow it outta my pipe!"

Not amused, Lewis said firmly: "We must come to a decision."

"We must?"

"It's only earth and plaster, this wall. I could fix it up again myself."

"Repeat the question to me," asked Slattery, serious also.

"Shall we pull the pipe out of the wall?"

"No, the real question."

"What?"

" 'How did you learn these abilities?': repeat that."

"What?"

54

"Repeat: 'How did you learn these abilities?' "

His face softening, Lewis asked: "How did you learn these abilities?"

"With time . . . yes, with time . . . and a love for my materials. Now that you have decided to take up paintin', Arthur, let me give you a few . . . pointers: if you do figures, face them toward the center . . . toward the sun. Paint some greys somewhere . . . blue-grey . . . black-grey . . . yellow-grey . . . red-grey. For contrasts. Always. In texture too. Above all, slip in, but not too obviously, a touch of similar . . . yes similar . . . color . . . in each corner. A touch. Get it?"

"Thank you."

"Many would give their lives to know. Similar colors in each corner."

"Yes."

"Francisco knew."

"Yes."

Slattery rose to his feet, held up the bottle to Lewis, thrust it into Lewis's hands.

"Now then."

"Yes."

"Let's get at that pipe."

"Wait a minute," said Lewis.

"What?"

"I know you're a good painter. I know that!"

"What?"

"Here's to you." Lewis raised the bottle and drank.

Slattery looked for a moment in silence, then with a massive shout of laughter he rushed toward the toilet, planted his feet against it, caught hold of the top of the lead pipe, and with a single pull tore it out of the Spanish wall.

In the living room the sleeping boy still lay on the sofa. The pipe was stretched across the radiators.

"How old are ya?"

"Fifty-three."

"Fifty-three. Fifty-three! Jesus."

55

"How old are you?"

"I'm not tellin' ya."

"Older than me?"

"Yeah. Older. A year or two older. Yeah, three or four years older. I was the first American to run four ten. Unofficial. The coach held the watch. Then I won at the Garden. How hot's that pipe?"

Lewis rose from his chair, felt the center of the pipe.

"Warm. Getting hotter."

Lewis returned to his chair.

"I won, but I never did four ten again. Let's get to it. I've been waitin' long enough. Let's get to it."

"Get to what?"

"What's your problem? What's your problem with the wife?"

In the silence that followed the question Lewis kept gazing at the pipe.

"It's got to come out. You've been wantin' to tell me. And I haven't been wantin' to know."

"Now you're ready to know?"

"Yes."

"Why?"

"You've seen my work. Haven't you? You've seen my work."

"Yes, I have. I'm glad . . . I'm glad you can paint. I'm glad you're such a good painter. That's the best thing about all this."

"What d'ya mean?"

"I mind, you know. I mind about your painting."

"That's not what I asked ya."

"I've not known a . . . a creative person before."

"No?"

"No."

Lewis lit a cigar.

"Anythin' you tell me I keep to myself."

"I know that."

"Even when I'm drunk."

"I know that."

"But I reserve the right to make comments."

"Of course."

"To you alone."

Silence.

Slattery took another drink. "For Christ's sake, get it out of ya, will ya? I know once you get started you won't stop."

"I suppose," said Lewis, "it's all to do with this sense of failure. I never had any power or drive. If I had I should have been offered a job at the Foreign Office. As it was I came back to England having had my chances, and failed to profit by them. For some time then, people I knew looked upon me as a might-be. Now I am not even a might-have-been."

"Jesus," said Slattery.

"If you interrupt me, I won't be able to tell you. I have to tell you things in my own way."

"Yeah, I see that," said Slattery after a pause. "All right, I'll keep my mouth shut."

"Most mornings I wake up feeling something horrible has happened. But I ward it off. I don't want to be dreary all day. There's nothing worse than that. I do try to be good company whatever I feel, with you or my wife or whoever. And I keep dreaming my first wife has died, although as far as I know she's very well . . . but I keep dreaming that."

"Your first wife?"

"My Indian wife. My brother says she still burns candles for me in Delhi."

Silence.

"My brother stayed."

Silence.

"So I left India and I tried to get into the Foreign Office, but when that turned out to be no good I just mooned about. My brother's always said I'm a softy. My brother's always said I had no self-assertiveness whatsoever.

"Patrick, I don't think you quite realize how much your eccentric side worries me. I worry about you. This dual personality of yours."

Silence.

"I loathe it when you're unhappy. Just as I loathe it when I'm unhappy. Or my wife now. Or even my first wife in Delhi. I

57

often think of her there in Delhi lighting those candles. One feels wretched when one looks back on one's life. I don't seem to know what's required. I never can help those I love when they're unhappy. I don't seem to have the knack for that. And you see it's when those I love are unhappy that I am at my unhappiest. Then I am left ashamed and wretched and don't know what to do with myself. You have talent . . . you are creative . . . when I say there are two sides to you . . . good and bad, if you like . . . kind and cruel . . . when I say this, it's the first that I cling to, and though the latter frightens me I can accept it as the inevitable counterpart of someone who is remarkable . . . or creative . . . especially after seeing your paintings today. But there is nothing remarkable about me at all. I shall never paint. I shall never write a book. My career . . . my dip-lomatic career finished fifteen years ago. I shall simply get balder and fatter and more tired. No one should be successful until they are old. Any success I ever had was when I was young. Now there is only failure . . . failure and old age. And in my youth I killed a boy.

"I get so tired, Patrick, that's the trouble. I find myself just able to look at things . . . things in the garden or out of the windows . . . or go for a ride . . . or go for a drive."

"Tell me when I can speak, for Christ's sake," said Slattery.

"Not yet. I might have been a good father . . . even now I think that . . .

"My wife . . . my present wife is young."

Lewis turned his head and looked directly at Slattery.

"You see, Patrick," said Lewis, "I have a wife who is young and beautiful."

3

"The climate down there, they say, is even more notorious for its extremes than our own joint."

"So I understand."

Lewis drove in dark glasses and a balaclava, with his coat collar turned up and thick woollen mittens over his hands, but Slattery sat with no coat in a cream Irish sweater and didn't seem to be feeling the cold at all.

They descended the hill. They saw the spires.

"Stop," said Slattery.

"What?"

"I gotta collect myself. Thank you for gettin' back my dollars."

Lewis looked into the rearview mirror, braked, and pulled over to the roadside on the brow of the hill.

Slattery gazed down at the stone lacework of the spires.

"It's good of you to bring me."

"That's all right."

"I'd never have got here on the bastard train."

They proceeded down the hill into Burgos, drove round the winding turn, were whistled ahead by the policeman, crossed over the bridge, glanced at the snow on the riverbanks, and passed through the medieval gate into the cathedral square.

Half the winter moon was still in the sky to the left, to the northwest of the main tower, as the bells and clocks struck eleven.

They got out of the Alvis, bought a ticket for parking, looked above at crows and doves astride the white horses, at the grey, black, and white stone mass, at the rose window, crossed the

59

street; and walked up the wide, worn paving with the pale sun on their backs.

In the cloister gardens on their right monks stood with folded hands in the damp green shade where no snow was, in the pigeon droppings, stood and whispered, their breaths misting.

They entered through the side door, took three or four steps, and stopped.

They breathed incense.

Walking, reading, praying priests went by, went south in white linen, and on echoing feet.

They stood still.

Young nuns went by with their fathers on their arms.

Somewhere, late, the fly-catcher clock struck eleven and echoed.

Both of them laughed: their laughter echoed.

They walked to the Christ in the green shirt in the crypt and Slattery crossed himself but Lewis did not.

They walked to the two candles before the gold baroque. "Our two souls," said Slattery. "I haven't got one," said Lewis. "This incense is chokin' me," said Slattery.

The cleaners came out of their cubbyholes behind pillars; a bearded old white-haired man in purple surveyed them and passed on. They continued. They came to a staircase and a balcony which led to a tapestry. They continued again. Every so often they were forced to look above.

A hard-voiced dignitary began: *"Dominus vobiscum.* Then the chant of the conclave in the center rose from the great choir seats and they hurried to the cold brass pillars and poked their heads surreptitiously among the pillars in order to see. In walnut stalls two layers of priests rose and fell, sat and stood, stopping and resuming their chanting, crying Amen and Amen and Amen.

But they were not allowed into the *coro* by the white-haired, bearded old guard in purple, who stood at the gate of the grille, raised a finger at them, and admonished with sunken eyes.

So they stood there by the paintings of Juan Rizi until the two layers of priests stopped their chanting, sat in their ornamented seats, and bowed their heads in silence. Some facing forward, some facing back.

Incredible that central dome, the vastness, the smell, and the gloom.

They stood there until the place was too much for them; then they hurried out to blink in the pale sun, both of them tripping over the step as they re-entered the light. Rubbing their eyes they descended the worn steps to the square, stopped, looked back at the rose window, looked at the pale sunshine filtering through to the grotto within.

"It's as she said."

"As who said?"

"My mother. My mother came here. Didn't I mention that?"

"No, you didn't," answered Lewis.

"That's why we came. 'Makes Chartres seem like a country church,' my mother said."

Over the two high towers the doves were circling and gleaming.

"We never saw the chest."

"The chest?"

"She told me the Cid filled his chest with sand and pawned it for a million to the Jews of this joint."

"Your mother?"

"My mother."

"When did she come here?"

"Before she was married."

To Lewis's astonishment, Slattery burst into tears.

"Whatever's the matter?"

But Slattery would not, or could not, answer. He stood there in the square with his shoulders hunched, his fists clenched, and he wept.

"Turn of the century . . . turn of the century she came here, my mother did."

Above, the pale sun turned into a jellyfish and submerged. The sky turned grey. Snowflakes fell upon them.

Lewis took Slattery's arm and led him across the square to the restaurant behind the hedge.

61

When they got inside Lewis asked for a fire for their feet and ordered brandy.

"She came here before she was married to my father."

They swallowed quickly: Lewis ordered again.

"Let's eat, for Christ's sake."

"Yes, let's eat."

"Her old man was a traveling salesman. *Chuletas. Chuletas por favor. Muy hecho.* Yeah, they traveled. Distract me."

"What?"

"Tell me about the little wife."

"Well . . ."

"For Christ's sake," said Slattery. "No half measures from now on. For Christ's sake, distract me."

"I can't."

"I'm beggin' ya."

"Patrick," said Lewis gently, "I can't turn myself off and on like a tap."

When they came out, warmer, the snow had stopped falling, lay clean and white on the steps before them, and although overhead they could not see the sun itself, here and there the sky had parted so that great furrows and ribs of yellow and gold and blue broke up the grey like banners. Again Slattery hesitated, to stare sadly at the cathedral as if it were a tomb. Beside him the wind blew over the hedge and powdered his grey hair white.

"Don't let's get cold."

"No, let's get home, let's get to *our* joint."

They walked in silence to the Alvis, both anxious now to be gone, with a sack of Burgos cheeses on Lewis's shoulders and Slattery humping Carlos Primero, both rolling and unsteady, sinking a little at every step.

But Lewis felt securer once they had climbed the hill, the heater warming his knees. Now Lewis *was* able to talk, able to distract. Now he wanted to.

Lewis had never known his engine run so well, and the car so quietly. He had never felt such a deftness at the wheel. He was in a ship, and steering before the wind.

When he wished to he could look away from Slattery, look ahead, because he was the driver, because he was in charge.

He could look ahead at the flat planes of snow on the cedars, the spikes on the tops of the cypresses, the clenched white gloves on the firs. He could watch the white chimney smoke drifting over the mesa like clouds.

As they left the little woods behind and entered the white desert itself, Lewis felt particularly at ease, felt borne along and enclosed.

"Of course," he said, "in our youth there was no youth. We had no money so we didn't matter. Our government was anti-everything. Anti-Democratic, anti-Semitic. Everybody that mattered was on the side of the Fascists, though naturally they didn't want any Fascists in England. Right and Left meant something then. Not like now. All my nicest friends became Communists, though none of them are now. But I was too modest for either side. What a fool! That was when I was at school.

"I don't think the young are any different now; it's just the conditions that are different . . . but they seem quicker to learn, more confident. They do much more what they want."

"Keep your eye on the road, won't ya."

"Don't worry."

"This ain't no hearse."

"That young boy . . . that boy on your sofa . . . what happened to him?"

"I fucked him," said Slattery, "I fucked him and then I threw him out."

But not believing Slattery, and knowing that sooner or later he was going to speak of his wife, Lewis continued as if he hadn't heard this answer: "Yes, I wonder what's happened to that boy. This new generation I have observed a little. They are interesting. I read about them and I watch them on the coast. I watched them all last autumn in Torremolinos. My wife loathes them. Can't stand their dirtiness. But it doesn't seem to bother me. They don't object to being called mindless, you know. They don't see why one should be anything else."

63

"I am waitin' for you to get to the wife."

"Yes, but this generation is interesting because neither work nor culture concerns them, neither intellectual nor material . . ."

"For Christ's sake," said Slattery, "speak of somethin' else, will ya? I know you see yourself in them, I know that."

"But what is interesting is their inability to campaign even for things that concern them: they know nothing about society and power. I mean since they believe that sensation is the only thing that matters in life they can't . . ."

"Stop it will ya. Speak of your wife for Christ's sake."

"But you see, what I wonder is how do you convince, how do you show . . . I mean you like young people, don't you?"

"*You* drink, they smoke pot. You look at television, they look at colored lights. You're cryin' vengeance because you're so alike."

"No, no, that's not it at all. What I'm asking you is how do you show a solipsist he's wrong?"

"A what?"

"A solipsist."

"I don't know," said Slattery after a pause.

The car went quietly and powerfully upward.

"I believe they're going Aztec and Arabian this year, Patrick. That's what I heard."

It was in the main street of Lerma that Lewis asked in a low tone: "Do you think that if a fairy tale is fulfilled it would be awful?"

"What?"

"Do you think that if what went on in your mind actually worked out it would be disastrous?"

"What kind of goin' on? Whose mind?"

"Night things."

"Night things!"

"Things at night."

Expecting some sardonic comment from Slattery, Lewis was pleased not to receive one. Glancing quickly over, he saw that Slattery frowned.

"Keep your eyes on the road, will ya."

"I mean what if a night fantasy became real. What if one made it real?"

"Disaster," said Slattery.

"But what if one got to the point when one had to find out?"

"Keep your eyes on the road for Christ's sake."

"Yes, but what if one got to that point?" asked Lewis. "What if one got to the point where one just had to go on?"

They crossed the Arlanza bridge.

"Let fantasy remain fantasy," said Slattery. "Let fantasy stay where it is."

Neither spoke again until they reached Aranda de Duero. There, Slattery sat forward in his seat and said: "I was once workin' in a road gang. There's a kind of powder you need for that . . . boric . . . these creams they're no good. I didn't know that then: after five days of it I got a terrific itch around the crotch. Couldn't change my underwear. Didn't have any to change. The heat was murder. Five days of it outside New York in August. Jesus. I came into town at the weekend and I had to have a woman. I finally found one in a bar on Forty-second Street. A young woman. She took me to her place. Her husband was in Europe. After I laid her, which was all right, she was still sleepin'. I got out of bed and picked up her panties. They were pink. Silk and pink. I held 'em up to the light. I put 'em on. They were cool. I threw mine into the toilet. I crept out. I dressed in the hall. I put on my shoes in the elevator. Christ! They were so cool, Arthur. In those days it was silk. In the forties. Now it's all nylon. That night . . . that night I got loaded. Fell into some . . . fisticuffs. With a Jewish guy. They picked me up. In the jail they stripped me. They stripped me and they called my father. They called my father in Boston. 'Fuck him,' my father said. I heard that. 'Fuck him.' 'He's standin' here in a woman's pink panties,' they said. That's what they told him: 'He's standin' here in a woman's pink panties.'"

"How awful."

"They sent me into the cells like that."

"But you see," said Lewis as they ascended again, "almost

65

every night now with my wife, I mean when I'm in bed with her . . ."

"How many times do you do it?"

"Oh only once . . . usually I can't manage . . ."

"I mean how many times a week? How many times a month?"

"Well, that depends . . . it goes in phases."

"You've reached the change of life, I don't doubt."

"Do men have that?"

"So they say."

"I mean sometimes quite a lot, some weeks not at all," said Lewis. "But when I do, when we are . . ."

"Fuckin'."

"Yes, fucking. Or just before."

"Or just after."

"No, never after. Then I just lie there. And sometimes I'm happy and sometimes I just think. But anyway, what I was going to say was . . ."

"D'you think a woman's magazine would sell?" asked Slattery. "Playgirl. Lot of men with big dicks? D'you think we should start a woman's magazine? Would it sell or wouldn't they buy it?"

"Patrick," said Lewis, "when I'm in bed at night with Jean . . ."

"Jean."

"Yes."

"What a horrible name! Jean, eh."

"When I'm in bed with Jean now . . ."

"I thought she was upper class."

"Oh no."

"I thought you met her at Cheltenham. Cheltenham Ladies College. I thought you told me that."

"I met her at Cheltenham but she was on an excursion. She was a waitress. She comes from Dalston."

"Dalston?"

"That's in London," said Lewis. "She worked in a café in Dalston. She came to Cheltenham on a bus tour."

"Jesus, I got it all wrong."

"So when I'm in bed with her now . . . I mean do you ever have this . . . I never did with my first wife . . . nor the girl I first lived with . . ."

"The girl you first lived with?"

"I must tell you about Jean, now I've got to it."

"Was that first girl friend upper class?"

"Oh yes, she was."

"Called?"

"What?"

"What was she called?"

"Virginia."

"What?"

"Virginia."

"She must have been upper class!"

"She was very promiscuous," said Lewis sadly, wiping the steam off the windshield with the back of his mitten. "That was what she was."

"All right, then," said Slattery. "Let's take them in order, let's deal with this Virginia first."

"I don't want to do that."

"Since we've begun, I know it will be best."

"I see."

"Was your father kind to you?"

"What? Yes. Oh yes."

"My father beat me like a dog."

For a minute or two the bends in the road grew so sharp and the surface so treacherous that Lewis was forced to concentrate on driving, but when they entered a straight again he asked: "You had a bad time of it, did you?"

"I was a dog."

"What I remember most about Virginia," said Lewis, "was in London. Right after the war . . . before I decided to go back to India . . . before I married Sharmini . . ."

"Sharmini?"

"My Indian wife."

"Only decent name of the lot."

67

"Yes, well when I was knocking around with Virginia I didn't care about her at first . . . I enjoyed her company . . . she was so young and pretty , . . she was very easy to sleep with . . ."

"She always came, eh?" asked Slattery.

"Yes, she always seemed to do that. Well, anyway, I wasn't in love with her or anything but we did become engaged, and then one night at a party a friend of mine . . . a great big fellow . . . a gentleman-farmer from Norwich . . . came up to me during this dance and he asked me if I happened to have any spare Frenchies on me . . ."

"Frenchies?"

"Don't you know what they are?"

"No."

"Are you joking?"

" 'Course I'm not joking."

"Well, they're contraceptives."

"Rubbers!"

"Yes, I suppose so. Yes, rubbers. Well, anyway, this man, Tim Fraser, came up to me and he asked me if I had a spare Frenchy. I was a bit drunk and laughing and I asked who it was for and he said 'Ginny.' I didn't mind at all . . . then . . . and I gave him one, but three weeks later I fell in love with her."

"So you gave him a Frenchy for Virginia?"

Lewis glanced over at Slattery, but Slattery was staring ahead so Lewis continued: "Yes, it was funny, really. I took her out on one of those paddleboats one day, down the Thames from Windsor, a lovely sunny day. We were laughing about everything, looking at the sailing boats, the punts, the motor launches, the pretty lawns on the banks and the pretty gardens full of flowers and suddenly I fell in love with her. That night we stayed together in a hotel in Bray. Monkey Island Hotel."

Without comment, still staring resolutely ahead, Slattery wiped the neck of the bottle of brandy with his hand, passed it over to the driver: Lewis took it and drank.

"Yes, that day I fell in love with Ginny. I don't know why. I

68

think it was mostly her smile. It was such a pretty day. She used to slide away from me to the bottom of the bed in the top sheet, you know, holding it round her like a fur coat, wiggling a bit and laughing."

"After a while you'd fuck her again."

"Sometimes. Sometimes I couldn't. But she never minded. Awfully nice girl."

"Yes."

"But from that day . . . from that day I was never happy unless . . ."

"You were fuckin' her," said Slattery.

The snow blew across the road in front of them in gusts. It whirled up and around and past in many directions. Lewis slowed the car.

There was no noise but that of the car engine; the car seemed to be on runners.

Except for the trunks of the pine trees everything in front of them had turned white.

"Yes, as you say, I lived only for the next time I could get her into bed. As soon as she was putting her clothes on I started planning the next time I could get them off. I thought of nothing else. That was the only time I felt happy . . . the only time I was happy was when I was coming."

"Or she was."

"Oh yes. Oh yes, then too. That was marvelous."

"What pain it all is," said Slattery.

"A week after I fell in love I started having nightmares."

"Yes."

"Night after night I dreamed she was lying on a bed naked, and all sorts of hands . . . his hands . . . Fraser's hands . . . would come floating out of the air plucking at her . . . plucking at her cunt like a bloody harp. Yes, even when she was lying in bed beside me!"

Slattery did not comment.

"It was horrible," said Lewis. "And I'd cry and she'd put her arms around me and try to comfort me. She'd say she was sorry. She'd say it meant nothing. Nothing! But I never got over it. To

69

think that I had been the one. And it didn't mean anything at that party. A year later when I met him, Fraser, I had to go into a lavatory and be sick. She did the best she could with me, Ginny, she really did, but she could never understand how deep the pain went. The pain hardly ever left me. I'd wake up and it would be there. I had other girls . . . but that didn't help at all. I'd always be thinking about her anyway. I knew it wasn't right to keep talking about it . . . to her . . . but I couldn't stop it. She was awfully good you know. Sometimes she'd get angry, sometimes she'd just laugh and sometimes she'd cry. But whatever she did I could see this man . . . her and this man . . . and in the end she left me."

"Yes."

"I don't think she fell in love with *him*. Even now I like to think it wasn't love. She just met this chap who was very kind to her."

"Kind?"

"A station master."

"A station master?"

"She married him. I used to write but she didn't answer. Then I telephoned. In the end I went back to India. I believe they've a lot of children."

"Yes."

"I don't suppose she ever thinks of me now."

"What?"

"I don't suppose Virginia ever thinks of me now."

"My father used to beat me with a wet towel," said Slattery.

"I wonder if she does ever think of me," said Lewis.

They had now reached the thick of the snows on the summit of the Guadarrama, at Somosierra; the wind howled in at the corners of the roof and Lewis slowed his Alvis and peered through the driving snow and weaved about in the middle of the road looking longingly ahead, both to left and to right, for one of those mountain cafés with a bar in it.

"Dos cafés, con leche doble, por favor."

"They do it also with rubber hose because it doesn't leave marks. Behind the knees. He'd get me up in a chair, knees bent

70

beneath me, hands clasped behind the head, he'd put the chair at an angle."

They sat with their backs to the radiators. They stamped their feet. They held their hands around their coffee glasses.

"You see those Anglo-Indians are very complicated, full of difficulties. Sharmini was all Indian. The family didn't like it. I thought I was right at the time. My father was very upset."

"But he didn't beat you with no hose."

"No, of course not."

When they came out the air was still. The pine trees stood motionless, leaning over at the angles the winds had grown them. A large round white moon rose over one mountain, a pale pink sun set over another. It seemed to Lewis that with one leap both sun and moon could be reached, that he could hang up there, a hand upon each rim and float without harm, while Slattery painted him. By the time Lewis had crossed the road and reached the car and looked up and down and about him, such was the sharpness of the air and the brilliance of the light that he felt himself weightless, transparent, and wondered while he fumbled for his keys if there was really any need to unlock the doors of the Alvis since he and his friend were now two ghosts, and could glide within.

"Hurry up, it's cold," said Slattery.

They rolled down the hillside in silence until the heater warmed them again. On this side of the hills there was no snow.

"Have ya got your lights on?"

"No, I haven't."

"Take it easy, will ya, kiddo."

"I'm not going fast."

"You ain't Fangio."

"I'm a very good driver," said Lewis. "You should know that by now."

Passing the moats and the walls at Buitrago, Slattery asked: "If I wanted you to keep somethin' safe for me would you do it?"

"Something safe for you?"

"Just a suitcase. You could keep it in your house."

71

"Why, exactly?"

"I don't want it around my place. Keep it out of sight of the wife, will ya?"

"Yes?"

"I don't want her openin' it!"

"Supposing she does."

"What?"

"Jean's in charge of the house. She knows where everything goes."

"Jean does?"

"Yes. She's the housekeeper."

"What about the basement?"

"The basement?"

"Don't you keep your empty suitcases down there?"

"But sometimes Jean goes down there. I could put it on a beam in the garage. Put a tarpaulin over it."

"I don't want it lost."

"No."

"I don't want it stolen."

"Of course not."

"Is your garage damp?"

"Yes, a bit."

"I don't want my suitcase lost, or stolen, or damp."

In the moonlight the plain before them stretched ahead in a peculiar vivid black.

"So Jean's the housekeeper, eh?"

"Yes, she's learned that."

"But not upper class, eh?"

"No."

"I'll think about this suitcase."

"All right."

"I don't want no one openin' it. You follow? No women."

"Well, what's in it, then?"

"Mind your own business."

"I'm sorry."

"Nothin' that would do you any harm."

"I see."

72

"I don't want nobody openin' my suitcase."

"I see."

"I don't want the *guardia* pokin' around in my suitcase."

"I see."

"Think of a place to keep it safe for me for Christ's sake. It's got photographs in it . . . photographs and pale pink panties."

As the drive continued some kind of anxiety began to build between them, as if both realized there was something yet to be settled before they reached Madrid. Both stared intently ahead, both were frowning, both smoked Lewis's cigars. When a cigar went out they lit up afresh.

Their feet were freezing.

Lewis began a tuneless whistle; Slattery wound down his window and held his head outside to the bitter air.

Black clouds crossed the white moon. They entered a rainstorm. Sheets of water lashed down upon them. The rain trickled in through the corners of the roof and fell on their knees.

Lewis swore but Slattery took no notice.

On the passenger side the windshield wiper stopped working.

A truck came blinding at them with yellow lights: Lewis braked too sharply and they skidded onto the verge; they cracked their knees.

Lewis restarted the engine, spun the rear wheels, jerked the Alvis back onto the road.

Slattery too started a tuneless whistle.

They got behind a trailer and could not overtake.

Then Lewis wanted a drink so Slattery uncorked the Carlos Primero and passed it over without comment. Lewis took it, bit the brandy back, and Slattery put the bottle away again in his pocket.

"You're sad, ain't ya," said Slattery at last.

"Yes."

At San Sebastián de los Reyes, Lewis pulled abruptly off the main road in front of a truck and bumped over side streets to a bar near the bull ring. He slid the car onto the ashes and got out. Silently, clumsily, Slattery got out also. Got out and followed Lewis into the empty bar.

73

Nobody there but the waiter and the black framed photos of wounded matadors: Arruza, Dominguín, Manolete, Ordonez.

"What'll you have?"

"Nothin', kid, I'm waitin' on you."

Lewis went to the bar, got a large brandy, and they sat.

"Another of your cigars, please."

Lewis gave him one.

Lewis was pale.

Lewis stared into his glass.

"All right, kiddo?"

Lewis raised his glass and looked into it. "It's terribly hard for me to begin," he said.

The rain blew in under the flimsy door.

"Sharmini, you know, was nothing. Nothing at all. Nothing ever happened.

"I always took a long time to come. She always came easily. Lots of times. Two or three times every night. But it was nothing. She was fat, jolly, and easy. I taught her to be clean. I must have cleanliness. I thought beforehand this would be the thing. I thought the responsibility would make a man of me. But it was too boring. We never had a cross word. Really she just lay there and came. Never chose a position. All the fantasies were mine. Everybody else was right. Every stupid thing said by every stupid person turned out to be right."

"Take it easy, Arthur."

"It grew unutterably boring. She was always lying there prepared. She never made one single positive movement. She was so kind . . . a whale. All she wanted to do was please. If I spoke to her she nodded her head. Her hands were warm, and wet, and absolutely accommodating. Drink made no difference, pain made no difference. She sapped me. She wore me out."

"Yes."

"Five miscarriages. Five placid miscarriages. The doctors loved her. I had her in a telephone booth while she spoke to her mother."

"Desertion?"

"Yes."

"Those were the grounds?"

"After ten years."

"Faithful?"

"Not even any need to check."

"Ten years, eh!"

"Yes. She ate and ate and ate. She bathed and bathed and bathed. She learned the Kama Sutra by heart. She got a new chin every year."

There was a long pause, then: "Anyone could have done it with Sharmini. Anyone."

Without being asked the waiter refilled Lewis's glass.

"Jean . . ."

"Yes."

"Jean seduced me."

"Yes."

"Jean came up to me."

"Yes."

"She came up to me and she said: 'I want you to make love to me. What's your name?' "

"Yes?"

"She was seventeen then."

"Yes."

"She was on an excursion to Cheltenham. It was in a pub I had. We used to cater for these coach tours. She was seventeen. She was a virgin. She stayed with me that night and she's never left me since."

"You got permission from her mother?"

"I did. I get on well with her mother."

"Poor old Indian woman."

"Yes. Have a drink."

"No."

"For God's sake have something."

"Coca-Cola, *por favor*," called Slattery.

The bells of a church rang out a local rhythm as if the monks were swinging on the bell ropes. Slattery's Coca-Cola was laid on the marble top; he lowered his head and sipped it. The pointed hands of the clock behind the bar were stopped and

75

rusted over. On the shelf above the clock the wine gourds were covered with dust.

Leaning forward on his elbows, holding his brandy glass in his hands, Lewis continued: "You see . . . what it is . . ."

"Yes?"

"What it is . . ."

"Yes?"

"Every night now when I'm in bed with Jean . . . I mean every night I'm making love to her . . . I keep wanting someone else to be there . . . someone else to help . . . not for me . . . for her."

"I don't understand you."

"Someone to help. Someone else to caress her. Someone as well as me."

"A threesome?"

"No. No! Not for me I said! For her. Someone extra."

"You mean someone to help you lay her?"

"She deserves the utmost. Jean deserves that."

"I don't quite understand you," said Slattery. "Am I being dumb?"

Silence.

"I don't exactly understand you."

Lewis stubbed out his half-smoked cigar in the ash tray, and lit another.

"Jean deserves it, you see. She deserves better than me. She deserves more than me."

"She does?"

"She's marvelous, you see. She's been everything to me. I have to be generous."

After a long puzzled pause, considering Lewis all the while, Slattery asked: "What does she say to all this? What does Jean say?"

"Well, she goes along with it at the time . . . in the nights. Of course I don't know what she really thinks of it."

"You don't speak of it durin' the day?"

"No, never. No, never, yet."

After another pause Slattery asked slowly: "Well . . . er

76

. . . well what exactly do you say to her . . . I mean when you're fuckin' her?"

"I told you."

"Yes."

"When I get excited I suggest other people should be there . . . I'm sure you know all about these things. You're the one for fantasies!"

"Never mind about me," said Slattery abruptly.

After a further long pause, not taking his eyes off Lewis, and frowning even more deeply, Slattery asked: "Who exactly? Who do you suggest?"

"Oh different people. Young people."

"Young people?"

"Yes."

"It's your age that's got to you, then!"

"They're always young people. People we've met. People we've seen."

"Both sexes?"

"No. No. Only men. I keep telling you. It's for her, not for me. One must face facts. That's the problem of life . . . to face up to the truth. That's the pain of life. Isn't it?"

"It is, eh?"

"Boys, usually. Sometimes I just make them up. I imagine some boy. Some unknown boy. A sportsman. A matador. Anything."

"Not El Cordobes?"

"No, not El Cordobes," answered Lewis without a smile.

"Never a girl?"

"I keep telling you, it's for her, not for me."

Three Spaniards entered the café, shook off the rain, nodded graciously, went to the bar.

"Mucha agua, señor."

"Sí, sí, mucha, mucha," agreed Lewis.

"Does what you say excite her?"

"Sometimes."

"Sometimes?"

"Sometimes I think it does. Other times I'm not sure. Some-

77

times she doesn't say anything. Sometimes she just laughs, and sometimes I don't think she does like it. Of course—" Lewis relit his cigar—"of course . . . well you see, she's never had the experience of anyone else. She's never slept with anyone else."

"And she never mentions it during the day?"

"I keep telling you. It only happens in bed!"

"Then leave it as it is."

Abruptly Lewis downed his brandy, went to the bar, got two, and brought them back.

"Please drink with me."

Slattery took the brandy, and nodded.

"I can't leave it as it is."

"Why not?"

Silence.

"I expect she just goes along with it for your sake."

"You do?"

"It probably bores the hell out of her."

"You think so?"

"I do think so."

"Patrick," said Lewis miserably, "I can't leave it where it is. I know I can't."

"You mean you've gotta have . . . have this for real?"

"Well, something."

"Something?"

"Something. You see I don't fuck her well enough. I'm fifty-three. Perhaps once or twice a week. But the other times I'm no good."

"It's time that's got to you."

Silence.

"Has she ever complained?"

"She wouldn't."

"How do you mean?"

"She's too nice to complain. Anyway, she's no other standards. She has no one else to go by. It's not fair on her."

"I don't know whether to laugh at you," said Slattery.

78

"You must do what you like," said Lewis. "What I'm telling you is the truth."

"As you see it."

"What I'm telling you is the truth," repeated Lewis.

Slattery drank his brandy, gestured for another cigar; Lewis opened his case, took one out, handed it over and lit it.

Slattery puffed.

"What exactly are you proposing then?"

"I don't know yet."

"A lover for her?"

"Perhaps."

"Two or three times a week?"

"Perhaps."

"Who'll choose him?"

"What?"

"Who'll choose him? You or her?"

"I don't know."

"You'd want to choose him, wouldn't you?" asked Slattery remorselessly.

Lewis took a deep breath.

"Wouldn't you?"

"Yes, I suppose I would."

"That would excite you, wouldn't it, Arthur?"

"I don't know."

"It's not as if she'd asked, is it, Arthur?"

"No."

"Let it stay in your mind . . . that's the place for it."

Silence.

"I might be much happier," said Lewis. "We all might be happier."

"I'm tellin' you, I know you," said Slattery. "I've seen this before. Don't ever do it."

Silence.

"You'll degrade yourself."

Lewis stared miserably away.

"You wanna become a fuckin' pimp?"

79

Lewis looked back at Slattery, who was leaning over the table toward him in his concern.

"Well at least I'm pimping for myself."

"You'll get so you're riggin' up mirrors."

"No, I won't. I'll go out."

"You'll want me to steal you a camera."

"No, I won't. I'll go out those nights."

"Those nights!"

"Yes . . . Patrick," said Lewis desperately, "I know I've got to do this. It's not a question of morality. It's a question of need."

"Need?"

"Don't be old-fashioned. It won't be the first time. Don't be such a bloody Puritan."

Silence.

"You've got to help me. You've just got to help me work something out."

"Maybe *she* can help you."

"What?"

"You haven't even spoken to her."

"No."

"Speak to *her,* then. Don't speak to me. I know where it'll end."

"She'll do what I ask," said Lewis.

"How do you know that?"

"I know Jean."

"Maybe she won't."

"Oh yes."

"Maybe she's got some sense."

"She's the kind of girl," said Lewis slowly, "who in this matter . . . and for me . . . will do what I ask."

"You're both sick, then."

Banging his fist down so hard on the table that Slattery jumped and the glasses fell on the floor, Lewis cried out: "Don't you understand at all? Don't sit there looking at me with that stupid concern and that pathetic suburban morality all over your face. I'm telling you this is real. What do you mean, *sick?* Sick!

80

That's meaningless. You of all people should know that. Why do you think I told you!"

"I'm sorry," said Slattery.

Waving a pacific hand at the barman and the other drinkers, Slattery rose, bent down, and picked up the fallen glasses.

"Will you take me home?"

"Of course."

"I wanna work, I've gotta work. I've gotta work now."

"Yes, all right."

"I'll pay."

Slattery paid; they left the café.

The rain had stopped and the stars and the moon were bright in the sky, but the wind blew eerily around the deserted bull ring.

"It's not that I don't want to help you."

They walked to the car.

"Shall we talk about all this again?"

Lewis answered miserably: "I know I'm going to need your help."

They got into the car.

"I must find the right person. The right boy. Not just for me . . . not just for her . . . for both of us."

Lewis started the engine.

"I can't go on like this, Patrick."

Lewis drove them back to Madrid.

4

As if it had just been put down out of its mold and polished, the building stood before them gleaming. Its top was crenelated like the turret of a castle; its aluminum-framed windows spaced evenly as portholes.

Letters of bronze announced: *Her Britannic Majesty's Embassy.*

"You're quite sure you want to do this."

Clean-shaven, sober, jaunty, Slattery laughed like a boy; careworn, stooping, Lewis sighed.

"Don't let sex defeat ya, Arty."

"Hmm."

"If your dick gets like an icicle you bathe it."

"Thank you."

"A dick is not an end in itself. A dick is a means to an end."

But Lewis stood unsmiling in that drab street of Edwardian office blocks and his country's strange circle.

"La Tortuga, the Spanish call it. Looks more like Dali's dream of a mushroom cloud ready for take-off."

Slattery led Lewis toward the black marble pillars, took him between the supports, to the center of the Embassy, to the small cascading fountain, to the glass-enclosed entrance up the circular driveway, to the *portero*.

The *portero* told them to go to the Consular section on the second floor, told them to go promptly because the Embassy closed at six.

"Don't be down, Arty, it's spring."

"I know that."

"How's your problem?"

"Just the same."

82

"Not passed?"

"No."

"Done anything about it?"

"No."

"Discussed it with the wife?"

"No."

"That's it, Arty, let fantasy suffice."

"Oh shut up," said Lewis. "I'm not in the mood."

On the second floor they turned left along a white impersonal corridor which reminded them both of a hospital.

"I don't want to talk about it."

"I'm sorry."

"Not now. Later perhaps."

It was the third door in the corridor which led to the Consular section. They entered. They found themselves in a small room with a counter, behind the counter a big office, and at the counter two solicitous Englishmen in neat grey suits.

"Do the talkin'."

So Lewis confirmed his inquiry: "Yes, Mr. Slattery, you can get married in our Embassy. All you have to do is establish residence for seven days. Then a clear fourteen days with the notice of your impending marriage on our board. Provided your papers, and your intended wife's papers, are in order, you have no problems whatsoever, Mr. Slattery."

"I'm sorry I was down," said Lewis. "Most unfair of me. I know you want to celebrate."

The red sun was falling behind the mountains but the air was still balmy.

"What about havin' some mussels? Mussels and a couple of beers. Then we could go back to my place and you can meet her. I'll cook dinner."

"Yes. Yes, we could."

"You'll like her. It's amazin'. A man goes all these years and then . . . it happens."

"I am sure I will like her."

"What about callin' up Jean and askin' her to join us?"

83

"Well . . ."

"Isn't it time I met her?"

"I don't know."

"I figure it's time. We should all meet. The four of us."

"I'll have to think about it," said Lewis.

Above their heads the birds still sang, the branches were green and budding; and everyone sat around them and drank in the warmth while the cars milled up and down both sides of the avenue.

They had to push through a crowd of Spaniards to get into La Ría.

"Great business. Always take you to the best."

Strings of mussels hung down the walls and in the green alcoves the black shells glistened. Young men and girls drank draft beer from glass tankards, sweated, ate with toothpicks, ate mussels, hot sauce, and creamed potatoes. Lewis sighed, sucked in his cheeks, and rubbed his tired eyes. But Slattery took Lewis's arm, smiled at him, winked at him, jostled him through that teeming place, bribed a waiter, got them a table, sat Lewis down, ordered for both, told Lewis a joke, and had Lewis laughing.

Like the Spaniards, they threw their empty shells onto the sawdust floor.

"No foreigners here," said Slattery with pride.

When they came out Lewis was still smiling.

So, not having been able to talk in the *mejillonera,* relaxed now, emerging into cooler airs, emerging into the Pasaje de Matheu, they decided to have coffee before making decisions.

"I stayed there once," said Slattery as they went by the Pensión Faustino. "That iron balcony was mine for a season." They passed windows: boys with white-tied shirts; a woman covered in her own black hair; a live toothless grandmother crushing up inkfish.

In a workers' bar—next to old men mending chairs in a step-up shop with basket beds and the window knee deep in caramels

84

—in the workers' bar over the black water gutter, through the black iron door, past the buttress, where no students sang and tourists never came, Slattery found them a corner among domino players, among Negroes, among old men, and there below the oak beams, with their backs to a yellow-tiled wall, Slattery ordered them coffee and mushrooms from a high-voiced waiter in a dark green jacket, and they waited, blinking because of the smoke from the open stove in the kitchen.

"You see, you're the only one I've ever told. And I don't think I'd like to sit there with her and someone who knows."

"I understand."

"You understand that, don't you?"

Slattery nodded.

"You haven't told anyone else, have you?"

"What do you take me for!"

"I mean not your . . . fiancée!"

"Of course not."

"Men do tell women they love."

The coffee was brought in a big brown jug.

"Here's to your marriage!"

"Thank you. . . . Have you told Jean you . . . er . . . you talk to me?"

"No. No. I just say we drink. I just say we drink together."

"That figures."

Slattery refilled their tiny cups from the earthenware jug.

"So if you were ever . . . ever to go through with . . . what you had in mind, you wouldn't want either party to know . . . either Jean or the young lover . . . the boy or whatever . . . to know."

"To know that I knew."

"Yeah. You wouldn't want either of them to know that you knew."

"I've been thinking a lot about that."

"It's still in your mind then . . . still all there in your mind?"

"More than ever."

The waiter brought the mushrooms.

"Yes, I've thought about that," said Lewis. "I decided *she* must know but he mustn't."

"Jean must know you know but the boy mustn't?"

"Yes."

"You'd arrange it and Jean would know you knew but the boy wouldn't?"

"Yes."

"He thinks it's a conquest?"

"Yes."

Slattery refilled the cups.

"You'd do the arranging?"

"Yes."

"You'd set it up?"

"Yes."

"You'd talk to her about it, get her agreement, and set it up?"

"Yes."

"But supposin' she doesn't agree to it . . . supposin' she wants no part of it?"

"I told you before I know she would agree. Somehow I know that."

"Yeah."

"If I really wanted it. She loves me. Jean loves me, you see."

As the commercial ended on the television set hanging over the black iron door, everyone else in the bar stood up for the bullfight.

"Supposin' she didn't find your . . . your helper . . . your protagonist . . . attractive?" asked Slattery. "That wouldn't be any good, would it?"

"I suppose not."

"So you might have more than one attempt?"

"Yes."

"Present more than one candidate?"

"Yes."

"More than one client."

"Yes."

In the bar the watchers of the bullfight booed and hissed. The

Negroes clapped their hands and whistled, the old men sneered, the old men spat.

"I mean I really haven't thought it all out . . . all the permutations," muttered Lewis.

"You'd play it by ear."

"Yes."

"Get her agreement, start one off and see what happened?"

"Yes. That is why it is so essential to start off with the right one. That is where I'd need your help."

"Jesus," said Slattery, frowning again. "Jesus, Arthur, why my help?"

"Because you're a judge of character."

In the bar the watchers of the bullfight cleared their throats and applauded.

"But you've not spoken to her yet?"

"No."

"Not at all."

"Well, I've sort of hinted."

"Hinted?"

"Yes, once or twice."

"And what was the reaction?"

"I don't think she's any idea what I'm getting at," said Lewis.

"You'll have to do more than hint."

"I will."

"Jesus," said Slattery again. "I was hopin' you'd abandoned it."

"No."

In the bar the watchers of the bullfight stamped their feet and cried *ole*.

"What would we look for? A boy with a big dick. A boy with a big clean dick. A big smart boy with a big clean dick? Or a big stupid boy with a big clean dick?"

"Don't put it like that."

"What other way is there to put it?"

In the bar the watchers of the bullfight went mad with joy and embraced.

"My one hope is," said Slattery, "my one hope is that if you

87

ever do talk to her she'll straighten you out. And anyway, sup-posin' . . . supposin' you brought it off and she got to pre-ferrin' the other. Supposin' she left you for the other?"

"That's a chance I have to take, isn't it?" answered Lewis.

In the air again they looked for a taxi.

"I think perhaps," said Slattery gently, "such bein' the cir-cumstances, we'd best leave Jean out of it tonight."

The avenues were still crowded, with all the couples walking, the traffic jammed at the fountains and in the side streets, so that their driver made slow progress across the city, braking, swear-ing, and banging his rooftop.

"So tell me about . . ."

"Françoise."

"Yes. She's French, is she?"

"Yeah. Father's dead. Stepfather's American. Lives in New York."

"Did she come over on a student's grant?"

"Too old to be a student. Stepfather pays."

"How old is she?"

"Thirty. Thirty-two. Maybe thirty-four."

"Has she married before?"

"No."

"Have you?"

"No. She's restored me. Her faith is touchin'. She tells me I'm the only man ever made her feel like a woman. She ain't no beauty but I adore her. Wears glasses. Writes me great letters."

"Where did you meet her?"

"Oh around. At a party. I got loaded. She looked after me . . . took me home. In the morning she was still there. They're usually gone. She's the only woman . . ."

"Yes."

"The only woman I ever had stay up there."

In the warm spring night Lewis opened his window and the oil fumes hit him.

"There's smog in this city now," said Lewis.

"She's studyin' the guitar. I've showed her my work."

"And she likes it?"

"Yeah. Yeah, she does."

Slattery went on talking while Lewis gazed out at the crowded city with the warm smog blowing into his face, feeling older than ever before.

"She's kind and she's loyal. Yeah, she's loyal all right. She's proved that."

"Is she a good fuck?" asked Lewis.

When they got out, and paid the driver, Lewis muttered: "I shouldn't have said that."

"It's what I've said to you."

"Yes. But you say things like that differently. What I said was nasty. When you say them they're not."

"Forget it," said Slattery. "I don't care." Slattery clapped Lewis on the shoulder. "Would you like to go on home?" asked Slattery. "I mean would you rather not come up?"

"No. No, I'll come up."

"She'd love to see you, I know that."

"You've spoken of me?"

"I've told her you're my friend."

Gratified, Lewis took Slattery's arm; they went into the hall and pressed the button for the elevator.

Opening the door of his apartment, grinning, Slattery shouted: "Francy! I've brought my friend Art."

There was no answer.

"Maybe she's in the bathroom. Are you in the bathroom, Francy?"

Françoise was not in the bathroom.

"Perhaps she's just run down to the store."

"Yes, maybe she has."

"Have a drink, then, eh?"

"Yes. Why not?"

They went into the living room.

While Slattery was pouring the drinks, Lewis wandered over to look at the two photographs on the mantelpiece—they had not been there when he was in the room before. The photo-

89

graphs were of two women, both bespectacled and smiling—one whom Lewis took to be Françoise, the other Slattery's mother when she too was in her thirties. There is no mistaking the likeness, thought Lewis.

Lewis grew confused; then, seeing the envelope on the corner of the shelf, he picked it up and took it over to Slattery.

"There seems to be a note for you," Lewis said.

No longer youthful, Slattery handed the note to Lewis, went to the sideboard, poured a brandy.

"I don't want to read it."

"Read it," said Slattery.

My own darling,

The door rang and I thought you had forgotten your key and it was you. But it was my mother. I didn't tell you I had written to her about our marriage. She has come from New York and found out where I was living. Because she is so upset I have gone with her to her hotel. She tells me that you are not allowed back in America or you will have to go to jail. I don't know how she knows this. I suppose my stepfather found out this. Why didn't you tell me? Does this mean we always have to live in Spain? I will come round in the morning. Mother is very upset. I know when she meets you everything will be all right again.

I love you, my darling. You know that. Try to sleep well. Don't get unhappy and drink too much. I adore you.

Your Françoise.

"She hasn't even put which hotel it is," said Slattery. "She hasn't even put the hotel! My Françoise hasn't even put the hotel."

Slattery gazed at Lewis, turned away in shame, let out some kind of cry, rushed across the room to the mantelpiece, picked up Françoise's photograph, and threw it out the open window.

They sat in a bar. The ceiling above their heads was sweating, they were surrounded by framed *toros,* the light bulbs were naked, the wine bottles were chained, there was football on the television, and the domino players were writing down their

90

scores upon the marble table tops. One of these players was crippled.

"What will you have?"

"*Sol y sombra.*"

"Oh no!"

"*Sol y sombra.*"

"But you'll see her in the morning."

"She should've waited till I got back. *Sol y sombra.* If you don't get it I get it myself."

Lewis rose heavily, went to the bar, asked for *anís* and cognac.

"*Dos?*"

"*No. Uno. Y una cerveza,*" said Lewis.

"I expect the mother's rather domineering," said Lewis.

Slattery did not answer.

Slattery downed his *anís* and cognac, looked contemptuously at Lewis's beer, went to the bar, and got himself another double.

"Why can't you go back to America? Is that bit about jail true?"

Slattery didn't answer.

"Is that bit true?" Lewis persisted.

"Yeah . . . I would've told her. I thought she wanted to live in Mojacar."

"Mojacar?"

"Gettin' a cottage there. Got a great view. Where's she wanna live? Beverly Hills. I hate America."

"Yes."

"I hate America."

"But what did you do?"

"What's it to ya?"

"I tell you things; you must tell me things," said Lewis.

Slattery emptied his glass and went to the bar again, returning with another large *anís* and cognac.

"Where's she wanna live? Long Island? Park Avenue?"

"What did you do?"

"A beatin' case."

"What?"

91

"I kicked a guy when I was loaded. When I get loaded I kick. I kicked one in Los Angeles. I kicked one in New York. I kicked one in Boston. When I get loaded I always go for field goals. Last time I jumped. I go back they'll stick me."

"I see."

"I can't stand no more of those county jails. Not in panties. Not any beatin' up in no panties."

"I see."

"They won't let me drink there. I don't want to be buried."

"I see."

"They kept puttin' me on probation."

"I see."

"Drunk and assault charges. They said I'm a disgrace to my father. That's a laugh. I always take a cab to jail, but last time I took one to the airport. Yeah, what they call a battery charge. Got any *fichas?*"

Another cripple entered the bar with one black boot and a black walking stick.

"Jesus," said Slattery. "Let's get out of here or they'll amputate us."

"Yeah, but what you haven't answered," said Slattery heavily, "is why she didn't wait till I got back. What's all this shit about the morning?"

"But if the mother was hysterical . . ."

"What's all this shit about: 'I will come round in the morning?'"

"Yes."

"What sort of people are they to check out on a thirty-two-year-old woman's fiancé?"

"Indeed."

"I'm the best lay she ever had."

"I'm sure you are."

"I'm telling ya I'm the best lay she ever had."

"Yes."

"I may be the *only* lay she ever had."

"Really."

"Her breasts have dropped."

"What?"

"Her breasts have dropped but I didn't mind that."

"I see."

"We were goin' to have babies and I wasn't gonna beat 'em. Give me some more *fichas*. I'll try the Hilton."

"Is that wise?"

"I figure they're at the Hilton."

"Why don't you wait until morning?"

"Por favor, hay teléfono?" said Slattery to the old woman. "If she had babies her breasts would rise."

"She's not at the Hilton."

"No."

"Nor at Luz Palacio."

"No."

"Nor at the Plaza."

"I see."

"Nor at the Commodore."

"No."

"I need more *fichas.*"

"Don't you think we should eat?"

"Are you suggesting I'm drunk?"

"Yes."

"Okay," said Slattery, to Lewis's surprise. "Let's go eat."

But in the taxi Slattery burst into tears.

"Would your Jeanny have done that?"

"Perhaps not."

"Your Jeanny would have waited, wouldn't she?"

"Their mothers are different, aren't they?"

"My mother would've waited. Nuclear bombs. People starvin'. Thievin', lyin', cheatin'. Who cares? Flame guns. She was my last chance, Françoise was."

"It'll all be all right in the morning."

"If I catch that mother of hers I'll fuck her."

Lewis smiled.

"Don't laugh at me!"

93

"I'm not."

"I'm tellin' ya, don't laugh at me. Would Virginia's mother have done that? Virginia's mother would've waited for you."

"Yes. I expect she would."

"When I get out I'll try the Velázquez. I'll try the Velázquez and the Wellington. I'll go in there and I'll lay the mother."

"What did ya bring me here for?"

"I thought the elegance might comfort you."

"You're hopin' to change my mood. You think I'm maudlin."

"I do think that."

"It's pathetic, ain't it."

"It is sad."

"Sad?"

"Yes, sad."

"I don't want your sympathy."

"All right."

"She ain't at the Velázquez or the Wellington. Ain't it pathetic?"

"Maybe they're with friends."

"A woman like that ain't got friends."

"Acquaintances then."

"Yeah, maybe. Yeah, you're right, I'm pathetic."

In spite of the Victorian elegance Slattery's spirits would not revive and only Lewis could eat: they sat in shirt sleeves over a faded carpet surrounded by noisy, happy, dark-suited Spaniards, and Slattery bowed his head and did not respond to the waiter's entreaties, staying politely for Lewis to finish, toying with another *anís* and cognac. Lewis thought it best to be silent and try to calm himself by appraising the room. Lewis put on his glasses and gazed over the bowed grey head at dark brown flowered paper, at the gilded ormolu clock, at rococo candlesticks, gold-beaded Empire pillars, gas-lamp chandeliers, silver goblets, silver candelabras, a marble fireplace, and terrible black paintings. "What a cruel world it is," Lewis murmured. Unable to comfort, like an antique dealer Lewis studied the prune-crested Victorian mirrors, the red velvet curtains, the solid gold curtain rails, the crimson velvet screens, the leather chairs, the silver trays upon the tapestried walls. When an American lady entered in a miniskirt Lewis was so unhappy himself that he got to his feet and totally uncharacteristically raised his glass and cried *ole*. This did rouse Slattery. Slattery raised his head and laughed. So, relieved but embarrassed, Lewis paid, and they slid across the polished hall like skaters, descended the spiral staircase, went through the cake shop below, and entered the busy street.

"Ah well," said Slattery, the air restoring him. "It isn't the first time."

"No," said Lewis, glad to be out.

On San Jerónimo that spring night at ten thirty it was still hot, the people were still carrying babies, the men still pushing and pinching. In the cake shop the people were stuffing themselves below pictures of milk shakes: stuffing meringues—*torteles, pinhas, imperiales, lazos, bambas,* and *bolas.* The old women sat in the doorways.

Lewis and Slattery went up a side street, turned a corner, entered a bar. In the center women were cooking in a glass booth. The roof of the bar had blue and green inlets. The soda siphons stood in chain-mail grids; the hatracks were horned; the paper napkins brittle. There were a million eyes in this bar—brown eyes, black eyes, green eyes. The ladies fanned themselves beneath their black arched brows, shook their strings of false pearls. The fat cooks in the booth disappeared in clouds of steam. *"Mucho calor* for the cooks!" Slattery went up to the glass and grimaced while Lewis fought for the drinks.

"Sol y sombra?"

"Sol y sombra."

They sat at a table and laughed at each other. They drank.

"The men in this town used to look at the boobs," said Slattery. "Now it's up the foreign minis."

"Only the toilet attendant has clean white lace," Lewis said. "Oh, the assurance of these fat female Spaniards."

"You'd like to make one leap?"

"I would."

"You'd like to be a gooser."

95

At first they were genial—they couldn't stop laughing—they kept patting the children; the little children with the tinseled sandals, the spectacles, and the wrist watches. They adored those fat female Spaniards; they despised the fat-stomached young men. Then Lewis wondered: "What about the Ritz?" As soon as he had asked the question Lewis realized that he shouldn't have.

"*Fichas*," said Slattery. "*Fichas*. You're right of course. The Ritz! She's a rich American Frenchy. She's a rich American Rubber."

"One-three-one," said Slattery when he came back. "Got through to the room . . . hung up when she answered."

"Who answered?"

"The mother."

"What are you going to do then?"

"Lend me your tie."

"No."

"Come on, I've gotta have a tie to get in there."

"No."

"I put your tie on . . . I walk right up there."

"Patrick, don't."

"I walk right up there and I speak in Spanish and they open the door."

"Please, Patrick."

"Maybe . . . maybe I can lay 'em both."

Sighing, Lewis handed Slattery his tie.

"I'm sure it's been done," said Slattery.

"And your jacket," said Slattery.

Lewis took off his jacket.

"See you around," said Slattery.

After Slattery left him, Lewis wandered. He could not go home to his wife. He wandered and drank. He found himself looking at a church with his hands clasped, as in prayer. He found himself on his knees like a beggar. He had forgotten Slattery: he had troubles of his own. At Siméons he stopped, pressed his forehead against the windowpanes, gazed at the lifeless women within, and began to court them. He enjoyed that.

He thought himself gallant. He could not understand why he was now so drunk. He knew he was staggering. He kept talking to himself and laughing. He kept talking to Virginia and his wives, asking their forgiveness. He found himself in a square he knew. An old square. He remembered the square as beautiful. They were turning the square into a parking lot. Lewis wondered if he himself had given the order and shouted out that he hadn't. He fell over hoses, girders, empty pipes, bricks, and wooden boxes. He found a chestnut tree cemented up in the middle. "So they mean to restore it," he said. "The liars." He kissed the tree several times and called it Jeanny. At the side of the square was a dark theater. He remembered that too as beautiful. He went to the glass doors and pushed them. *"Portero,"* he shouted. *"Sereno!"* The doors opened when he pushed, so he went within. *"Sereno!"* he shouted, but no one came. He looked at the statues in the foyer. He couldn't understand why the theater wasn't locked. He left the theater, went to the bar on the corner, bought a bottle of brandy, re-entered the theater. He passed through the foyer, between statues, and entered the dark auditorium. He sat in the aisle and opened his Carlos Primero. He sat there a long time, drinking. He didn't know why. He thought of Jean and heard himself muttering poems, love poems, poems of devotion, poems of tenderness. He became convinced that he too was a poet. "I love my wife," he kept calling. "I love her."

When at last he came out of the theater he had half finished the bottle. He emptied the contents over his shoes. "Good for the leather," he said. He found a taxi and gave his address in the Puerta de Hierro. Passing the university he saw policemen on guard and thought of Slattery again for the first time in an hour. When they reached his house he deliberately overtipped, and went into the garden. He lay down on the lawn. He slept a little. Then he woke. "The dew will get you," he said. "The dew will get you in the back. You're too old for the dew." He took out his key and went to the front door. He listened. He undid his shoes and entered, leaving them on the steps.

There were no lights within. He tiptoed to his dressing room. In the dressing room he switched on the light.

97

He could see his wife in the shadows; he could see his wife in their four-poster bed. "Darling," he whispered. "Darling." But she slept like a child.

He went to her. He kissed her. She did not wake. "Sleep well, my young love."

Then Lewis became fearful for Slattery. He left the bedroom, passed through the dressing room, went out into the garden again, found a corner like a dog, put his hand down his throat and vomited. He retched and he retched. He huddled himself on his knees and retched black vomit, and tears rolled down his face and his chest.

Then he went to the swimming pool and jumped into the water in his clothes.

Returning to the house he dressed in fresh clothes in quiet, left a love note on the table in the hall, came into the night again, picked up his shoes off the doorstep, put them on, went to the garage, got into the Alvis, and drove back to the center of Madrid.

Now he kept noticing how warm was the air and the smell of the blossoms.

Parking on the corner opposite the main entrance of the Ritz, Lewis wondered if Slattery was still inside: he looked at his watch. He could not be sure that Slattery had entered. Perhaps Slattery was now in jail. At any moment he expected a police-man to come up and question him but none did. He decided to sit there for an hour, then go to Slattery's apartment. He himself felt purged and strangely content.

He had no desire to smoke.

He sat there while the clocks struck and struck again.

What he kept wondering was why he so wanted to go on with his own intention, why he so wanted to proceed with his own plan. He knew now, definitely, that he would. Somehow this night had sealed that.

Between three and four Slattery came out of the Ritz, stopped on the pavement, took off Lewis's tie, Lewis's jacket, slung them over his shoulder, breathed deeply, looked up at the night sky, walked over to the railings, hung Lewis's jacket upon them, put his hands through the railings, and rubbed them on the leaves of a shrub. Blossoms fell. Lewis realized Slattery was rubbing his hands in the dew on the leaves. Lewis saw Slattery rub dew all over his face.

Slattery folded Lewis's jacket over his arm, put Lewis's tie into the jacket pocket, left the flowering bush, left the railings, turned north, and set off up the avenue.

Lewis waited a while, started the Alvis, followed Slattery, and caught him.

"I don't want to ride," said Slattery.

"Let me park the car and I'll walk with you."

"Okay."

Slattery waited while Lewis turned off the Paseo del Prado to park his car in the Calle de Montalbán.

"Want your jacket back?"

"Thank you."

"Tie's in the pocket."

"Yes."

They crossed the Plaza de la Cibeles and walked on north up the Paseo.

"Well, I did it," said Slattery quietly. "I did it, and that's that."

They crossed the Plaza de Colón.

Lewis had not spoken because there was a detachment in Slattery's statement which made Lewis feel there was nothing he could possibly ask.

They went up the Castellana.

"I thought I was jokin'. I *was* jokin'. I had no image of it. It had gone from my head when I went in there. But it occurred."

"What do you mean?" asked Lewis, wondering for a moment if the worst had happened and Slattery had kicked out, bit, or murdered.

"I did fuck the mother," said Slattery.

Lewis realized at once that Slattery was telling him the truth.

99

"At first it was funny. You know how drunk I was. I found the room and I spoke in Spanish. Francy opened the door. I guess she knew who it was. I came in and I shut it.

"The mother was in bed.

"They'd both been in the bed. It was a double bed. That's what they had there. A great double bed. Francy was wearin' a bra and her panties. The mother was wearin' a nightgown. I started to laugh, I took off your jacket, I took off your tie, and I got into the bed.

" 'Keep quiet,' I said, 'or I'll rape ya.' The mother started to scream, but I told her again, and she stopped it. Nobody came. Francy went and sat on a chair with her hands in her mouth. 'Come into bed, Francy,' I said. But she wouldn't. She just sat there. That's what Francy did. I don't know why . . . that stopped me laughin'.

"We started to talk. Francy sat in the chair, I lay by the mother. I asked for a drink. The mother had a bottle. Francy poured and I asked the mother if she wanted a swig. She kept talkin' in French, not American. To my amazement she took the bottle and belted one back. She's a fat woman. She ain't as tall as Francy. Francy put on her glasses. And I had another drink. The mother talks like Signoret.

" 'I love your daughter,' I said. That shook her. I could see that. She hated that. Francy took her hands out of her mouth and relaxed. 'I love your Francy,' was what I said to the mother.

"Then I told stories. I told a lot of stories. I charmed 'em. You know how I can do that. I told 'em about my father. Everythin'. All the time the mother's lying beside me. I told 'em about España.

"Francy's in the chair and I talked for two hours. Francy's got on her glasses.

"I'd drink, the mother'd drink. Francy would laugh. She'd look quite young.

" 'He's old enough to be your father,' the mother said. 'Say it in American,' I said. And she did. 'Patrick's old enough to be your father.'

"Then *she* started to talk. She hates her husband. I could tell

100

that. She hates America. She loves De Gaulle. She talks like Signoret.

" 'You're old enough to be her father,' she said. 'Patrick.'

" 'There's been others,' I answered. 'There's been singers and judges.' We were laughin'. 'There's been Sinatra,' I said.

" 'You're as old as me,' she said.

" 'So put your hand on my prick,' I told her.

"Then she looked at Francy . . . she looked at Francy, Francy, still in the chair . . . she looked at Francy, she threw off the bedclothes and she went right down on me."

They walked up the Generalísimo.

"I could see Francy, over her head. Over her blue-rinsed head. Francy did nothin'. Francy put her fingers back in her mouth and did nothin'. I didn't come. When she was through Francy was still doin' nothin'. So I pulled Mother up on top of me and I laid her."

"God Almighty," said Lewis. "I'm so sorry for Francy."

"She'll end up in a home . . . like all of us."

"How awful. How awful."

The two friends walked on up the Generalísimo.

"An' neither of 'em bid me good-bye," said Slattery. "Do you know that? Neither one of them. Are there any further details you require for your own enlightenment . . . are there any more details you require?"

They walked on and on.

"Don't think that woman didn't know what she was doing, Patrick."

"Don't think I don't know what *I* done."

They walked on.

"I thought she'd catch me by the hair. I thought Francy'd leave that chair and catch me. But she was frozen."

He couldn't have really loved her, thought Lewis.

5

Summer came. The reservoirs emptied. Madrid burned. No sprinklers were allowed on the lawns. The streets cracked, streets fell in; the rats went into the sewers for water. The tree trunks on the avenues turned brown; the sun fried the leaves of the scrub oaks, the poplars, the chestnuts, the broom, the sycamores, the forsythia, and the plane trees.

There was smog every night; prices spiraled; the traffic accidents trebled in number.

The rich fled; the poor took their picnic tables to the Casa de Campo and ate beneath umbrellas.

Only the builders remained; they tore down the palaces on the Castellana; they tore down the Larios, they tore down the Medinacelli. They dug up the Plaza Mayor. Even along the trickling Manzanares the housing complexes arose. Each ultramodern block spawned its own supermarket. Monstrous cranes hung over everything. Scraggy, spindled skeletons of steel fed into the horizon.

It was too hot for Lewis to play tennis with his wife; Slattery no longer could drag himself down to the Prado.

My dear Patrick,

How are you? Long time no see. Cannot stand the inferno any longer.

I am putting Jeanny on a plane to Málaga and following in the Alvis as I want to see the Alhambra again.

Would you care to accompany me and dip yourself in the Med? We are staying in Fuengirola. . . . What about your friend in Mijas? I would run you up the hill. And maybe we could have the odd jar now and again.

102

What do you say?

I could just put the roof down and off we go.

How's the work?

Will you call me?

If I don't hear from you I shall buzz and see you in the autumn.

Your friend
Arthur

In Granada they followed the arrows and signs, drove up the winding street, till they came to Wellington's elm trees.

The radiator boiled over again; Slattery's face was crimson.

"I should have brought some cream for that nose of yours."

Lewis parked, found a store, bought sun lotion and rubbed it on. Slattery said nothing.

"You're a stoic, aren't you?"

"Up my ass for a dollar."

They went through the first door of the first wall. The watercourses murmured all about them.

"I was wrong," said Slattery. "It was worth it."

"Isn't it beautiful?"

"Moist hands have been placed on my hot cheeks. Shall we wander?"

"I think so."

"I'll take the gardens, you take the interiors. When our paths cross we're strangers."

"I see."

"Have I hurt ya?"

"I just wanted to show you one or two things."

"Solitude is what I require. We ain't married, Arthur. Meet you in two hours. I don't require no guidebook."

"As you please," said Lewis. "As you please."

If Lewis had been upset he was soon restored. Going their separate ways they passed between columns, underneath arches, climbed up to towers. They stood among black bushes by green pools. They gazed at lacy walls and painted ceilings, tapestries and gold mosaics. They sat beneath glittering domes. They stared down ravines. They entered the Court of Myrtles, the

103

Square of Cisterns, the Hall of Benediction, the Hall of Secrets. When they passed each other they would nod—they nodded in alcoves, marble bathrooms, on balconies, and on battlements.

When at last they spoke it was on the hillside. They spoke with a landscape of gardens below, with roses, jasmine, cypress and yew trees around, within ocher walls, a blue sky above, and afar the golden Andalusian sun shining on the white peaks of the Sierra Nevada.

Lewis came out of the calm blue sea and threw himself down on the sand; with a grin Slattery levered himself off the rail of the boating-club pavilion and made his way among the bodies.

"Hi, sun worshiper."

Lewis sat up.

"Oh hello."

"There's a bar in Mijas . . . I'm there most nights. I eat *paella*. Best on the coast. A girl makes it."

Slattery set off.

"Wait a minute."

Slattery stopped; Slattery came back.

"I don't love it here. It's like a lido."

"But just a minute."

"Which one's your wife?"

"That girl out there on the catamaran."

Slattery shaded his eyes, followed Lewis's pointing finger.

"She's pretty."

"Told you that. Sit down. Sit down, take your shirt off."

"I can't. I burn. And I don't like sand up my asshole. Is that a candidate with her? Is that a client?"

"Sit down on this." Carefully shaking his towel Lewis laid it back on the beach.

"Sit on my towel."

Doubtfully Slattery did so.

"How long will she be?"

"Half an hour unless they row back. There's no wind."

"Is that a runner?"

"She doesn't like him, I'm afraid," said Lewis. "She says he's stupid."

"As soon as she comes, then, I'm off."

"Do you want a beer?"

"Get me a Coke."

When Lewis returned he found Slattery shading his eyes again and frowning out at the catamaran.

"He *is* stupid. You can tell that from here."

"Where is this bar in Mijas?"

"At the corner of the square."

"Any night?"

"Any night. I bet that's the kind of guy shaves his pubics."

"Really."

"What's she laughin' about?"

"I don't know."

"What's she laughin' about? You never told me she was pretty."

"I did."

"You never told me she was pretty. So pretty and so young. If she asks you who you was talkin' to tell her it was an athlete. Tell her I ran the mile in four ten at the Garden!"

Smiling, Lewis passed Slattery his Coca-Cola; smiling, Lewis began to drink his beer.

"I've trained myself to do without women. I should've done that years ago."

"You look thinner."

"I am thinner. I can't work here. I think I'll be goin' back."

"You can't work, eh?"

"No, I can't work. The light's different. I don't know why I can't work."

A breeze sprang up from nowhere, filled the sails of the catamaran, and blew it toward the beach: hurriedly Slattery got to his feet.

"I'm off then."

As suddenly as it had risen the breeze was gone.

"I take it you've dispensed with your . . . plan."

"No."

"No?"

"On the contrary."

"You didn't learn nothin' from me?"

"No."

"Why not?"

"There's no parallel," said Lewis. "None."

Regarding Lewis with a mixture of disbelief and irritation, Slattery sat down again upon the colored towel.

"You mean you learned nothin' from me, you idiot."

"No."

"I thought you'd gotten over it."

"No."

"You didn't mention it on the drive."

"I didn't feel like it."

"I was sure you'd gotten over it."

"No."

Looking carefully about him and moving closer to Slattery Lewis said in a low mutter: "I talked to her at last . . . I mean I talked directly . . . well, in a way, directly . . . she's so much younger than me . . . I told her if she ever wanted to have an affair . . . yes, as long as it wasn't thrust in my face . . . I wouldn't mind."

"You idiot."

"I told her if she did I'd understand."

"You idiot."

"Don't keep on saying that and keep your voice down, please."

"You idiot."

"There are people who know me here."

"There's nobody who knows you here," said Slattery grimly. "You saw how I loused up my life, didn't ya?" Slattery looked up at the burning sun, then out at the catamaran on the sparkling water. "What does your pretty wife say? What does that poor bitch say?"

"Don't speak like that about her."

"Okay."

106

"At first she laughed. Then she got upset. Then she tried to comfort me. We went away, you know, for two weeks. To the northwest. We'd never been there. The water's cold there but so much nicer there really. Really refreshing when you get used to it."

"But what did she say?"

"I'm telling you. Don't be so impatient. When we came back I kept on at her. She got confused again so she began to humor me. 'All right,' she'd say teasingly, 'I will find a lover.' But she didn't mean it. 'Who shall I have?' she'd ask me. But she never said anyone real. Nobody real."

"That's what I've always said. She don't want . . ."

"Then one night I told her," Lewis interrupted, "I told her—" Lewis hesitated—"I was like you, I suppose . . . I suppose I had to do it . . . I told her *I* had been having an affair."

Slattery said nothing; Lewis picked up handfuls of sand, let the sand trickle out between clenched fingers.

"I said marriage was ridiculous anyway . . . an impossible institution. I said fidelity was pointless these days. I said that wasn't what love was. I said fidelity wasn't what love was. I said if one really loved, one should let one's partner enjoy himself . . . as he wanted to . . . yes, I told her I'd been having an affair for months."

"So she batted you one across the face."

"Yes, she did," said Lewis. "That's exactly what she did. But I told her it's marvelous to have two people in the same day. I said jealousy . . . jealousy is the worst sin."

"So she belted you again."

"Yes. She was very fiery. Then she cried. Then she got very excited."

"And you laid her?"

"Yes, I did. Then she cried again. Then she hit me again. And so it went on. After that night she wouldn't sleep with me for a week. Then she did. 'Tell me it isn't true,' she kept saying. But I stuck to my story. I'd stay out late and drink somewhere and when I got home I'd tell her a pack of lies."

107

"You're mad," said Slattery. "That's what you are. You should be put away. You are stark ravin' mad."

"No, I'm not," said Lewis.

A look of extraordinary sadness came over Lewis's face.

"I don't want her to leave me," said Lewis.

They both gazed out at the girl on the catamaran.

"I don't want to die alone," Lewis said. "The conflict is necessary!"

There was no wind at all upon the water.

"This is the difficult stage, you see," said Lewis. "It's all a game. It's all a sort of game really. There's no rules. I have to do it like this to keep her. Otherwise . . . otherwise she will leave me. In the end . . . in the end I will be proved right. What I want . . . what I have to have must be permanent. I am striving for truth, such as it is. I am striving for love. I don't want just another marriage. You've no stamina except in your work. What I'm striving for . . . what I have to have is true love. I don't think you understand what a game it all is to get that."

"I'm gonna wait till she comes in," said Slattery. "I'm gonna tell her the truth."

"No, you're not."

"I'm gonna tell her you've gone nuts."

"She won't believe you. Anyway, I haven't."

"I'm gonna tell her you're a liar . . . she'll believe that. She'll *welcome* that."

"That would be a breach of our confidence," said Lewis.

The breeze rose up again, filled the sails of the catamaran and blew it fast toward the beach.

"Why don't you let *me* lay her?" said Slattery.

"She wouldn't."

"Why don't you let me try?"

"Because," said Lewis, "it's got to be somebody innocent."

Lewis stood up.

"You'd better be going."

The catamaran blew onto the beach: heavily, Slattery rose.

"Somehow," said Lewis, smiling ironically, "somehow I'd rather he was English or American. I don't want a Spaniard."

Lewis held out his hand, still smiling, but Slattery did not take it, and Slattery left the beach at Fuengirola without an answering smile.

The blue convertible gleamed and shook on the cobbles. The hot old leather was smelly. Above their heads washing hung down from the balconies—pink sheets.

Lewis glanced at his wife—she was still sleeping. He wanted to kiss her.

He accelerated past a garbage cart, raced out of the village up the avenue of brown and yellow trees.

He was longing to get back to the city.

He drove through a fertile circular valley around a hill—passing a team of oxen, passing a black diesel truck—as if he were in a race.

He sped through poplar woods and lime woods—the sunshine and the shadows flickering over her head.

He rushed onto the plain, with a great granite bluff on his right.

By the roadside they were gathering potatoes; the autumn air was balmy. While she slept Lewis drove faster and faster.

6

Autumn in the Café Gijón. Outside their window a group of nuns holding up the traffic. The car wheels muddy from yesterday's rain. No awnings over the tables in the center of the avenue, brown leaves on the drooping trees. Each old lady that passed glanced in at them; no women within at this hour.

"Another coffee?"

"No."

"What time's the appointment?"

"Twelve."

"Why are you so nervous?"

"Would you come with me?"

"Me?"

"Yes. Would you come with me, please?"

"Of course," said Lewis. "If you want me to."

Lewis looked at his watch, beckoned to the waiter for more coffee.

"I want you to do the bargaining."

"But I have no idea. I wouldn't have the vaguest notion what to ask."

"I'm takin' four: three hundred dollars each. Three-fifty for the big one."

"I see."

"They're my best."

"Then maybe I ought to ask more," said Lewis.

Lewis waved to the bearded shoeblack.

"You haven't got time for that!"

"Of course we've got time," said Lewis. "We've got ages. What are you so nervous about? It's only five past eleven."

110

"It makes me sick," said Slattery. "I've been through this before."

The shoeblack knelt at Lewis's feet on the red-and-white-tiled floor, put leather protectors in Lewis's shoes, began to rub. Lewis sucked in his cheeks.

"Is it a man or a woman I have to deal with?"

"A woman."

"Have you met her?"

"No, I wrote her a letter."

"I think I'd better ask more and come down. Don't you think so? I must leave myself some room to maneuver."

"They're all the same, I tell you that," answered Slattery. "They're shits."

"In that case I think I'll have a brandy."

"Go ahead."

"Will you join me?"

"I can't drink at times like this."

Lewis beckoned again to the waiter, ordered a large cognac. The bearded shoeblack finished the right shoe and began the left.

"I'm rather glad for the distraction, as a matter of fact."

"Yeah."

"I'm a bit edgy myself today."

"Why?"

Easing himself round to the window so that the warm sunlight fell on his shoulders, glancing quickly at the other customers in their glasses and their berets, Lewis whispered: "I've changed my tactics."

"I can't hear ya."

"I've changed my tactics."

"What tactics? Speak up."

"I can't speak up."

"Why not?"

"I don't want anyone to hear."

"Hear what?"

"What I'm going to tell you, you bloody idiot."

111

Slattery groaned.

"The old tactics didn't work, you see," whispered Lewis, leaning closer across the black-and-white-marble table top. "I've had to change them."

"I don't want to know," muttered Slattery. "Please," he implored. "You know I don't want to know."

"If you want me to come with you and do your bargaining," said Lewis, "if you want me to come and help you out with your problems you can jolly well listen to mine."

"Oh Christ," said Slattery. "All right, then. Get it over with."

"Well," said Lewis, looking around anxiously, moving even closer to Slattery, and sipping his brandy. "Well," said Lewis, paying the bearded shoeblack, "it's a young cousin of mine."

"Go and sit back on the other side of the table," said Slattery. "Nobody in here gives a damn."

"He's staying with us, you see," said Lewis, without moving. "I thought of him one day and I asked him over for a couple of weeks. I leave them together as much as I can. He's a very good-looking boy. She likes him. I can see that."

"That won't work."

"It won't?"

"Throwing them at each other like that won't work."

"It won't, eh!"

"I may be wrong," said Slattery. "With women I've been wrong. But I'm sure your little Jeanny knows what you're up to."

"She does."

"It won't happen with one of your cousins."

"No?"

"Not if they speak like you do."

Slattery laughed.

"It won't happen with one of your cousins," said Slattery sardonically. "It might happen with one of hers."

Lewis parked the car at the side of the Hilton Hotel and Slattery got out the paintings. Lewis saw that Slattery was nervous again.

112

"I've been thinking about what you said about my cousin."

"Please, Arthur, this is very important to me."

When they entered the beautiful townhouse off the Castellana, they found themselves in a shop, and were told to ascend. They passed by very expensive children's clothes, leather goods, lace supper cloths marked at six thousand pesetas, and marble eggs marked at three hundred and sixty pesetas—which Lewis well knew sold for ten shillings everywhere else. "It's a tourist trap," muttered Lewis. Slattery stumbled along behind with his paintings. I do wish he wasn't so anxious, thought Lewis. It doesn't make it any easier for me. Next time I'll come on my own.

When they reached the top of the marble staircase a hung-together American woman of forty with braided hair stood there in a skirt and a blouse. A lumpy woman; a woman plain and hard.

"Good morning, this is Patrick Slattery, the painter. I am Major Lewis. How do you do . . ."

"Weissberger," she said. "Mrs. Weissberger. Yes?"

"Mr. Slattery wrote to you, I believe. He has some paintings here he would like you to exhibit for him . . . the usual terms, of course. You asked him to come at twelve and here we are on the dot."

Indeed the clocks in the city were striking the hour.

"I don't remember any letter," the woman said.

"Oh." Lewis turned to Slattery. Slattery was pale and dumb.

"Well, now we're here," said Lewis, "now we're here . . . would you care to look?"

"Where else has he been hung?"

"What?"

"I said where else has he been hung? Where are his brochures?"

"Oh," said Lewis. "Oh. Oh yes. Patrick, have you exhibited your paintings elsewhere?"

"Fricker in Paris. L'Attico, Rome. Mills College Art Gallery, Oakland, California. De Young Memorial Museum, San Francisco. Marlborough Gallery, London," muttered Slattery, but so indistinctly that Lewis could hardly hear him.

113

"Not much of a list for a man of your age. Okay, open up."

After a moment, seeing that Slattery stood there so numbly, Lewis took the paintings from him, untied the cord around them, and displayed them for Mrs. Weissberger where best he could among the metallic ornaments of the one-man show already in the room.

She looked.

"Okay, I'll put 'em in the back room," she said, jerking her head behind her.

"The back room?"

"Behind me," she said. "Can't you see the door?"

"Oh there," said Lewis. "Yes, I see that door there. Yes. But how will people know if they're there? How will anyone know there's anything in there?"

"If I think anybody's interested I'll bring 'em out."

"I see."

Lewis looked doubtfully at Slattery, but Slattery was helpless. "Patrick?"

Slattery looked away from Lewis, looked from one to the other of his paintings, then without raising his eyes to Lewis or to the woman, without uttering a sound, he turned his back and went down the stairs.

"What are you going to do . . . leave 'em or take 'em?"

"What?"

"Suit yourself," she said, turning her back.

Lewis went to the door. Then he turned also. "Madam," said Lewis, "you are without doubt the rudest woman I have ever met. I do not know what you can sell, or what you cannot sell; that's not my province. I do know you are not the sort of person I would leave anybody's work with."

She seemed not to have heard.

Lewis went to Slattery's paintings. He picked them up. "There must be nicer people in Madrid," Lewis said.

She still had her back to him and seemed to be arranging something. She bent over a table.

Before he knew what he was doing Lewis hurried through the room toward the woman and with his free hand hit the woman as hard as he could across her behind. Then he fled, while she screamed.

But his rare mood of violence had left Lewis as soon as he reached the street. He found Slattery leaning against the Alvis.

"I didn't want that woman to sell your paintings. I didn't want to leave your paintings up there with that woman."

Slattery did not answer.

Slattery was silent all the way back to his apartment. Silent all afternoon. As far as Slattery was concerned Lewis might not have been there.

Slattery sat in his chair.

But Lewis stuck it out, and fed Slattery, and after he'd cooked the lunch he brought up the paintings from the Alvis and hung them up on the walls in Slattery's living room. Then Lewis looked at his watch, considered, took off his shoes, lay down on the red plush sofa, closed his eyes, and went to sleep.

Lewis was awakened by the sound of music. Still Slattery sat in his leather chair.

"That's the circus starting up," Slattery said.

"Oh yes."

Drawn to the window Lewis looked down at the children's carousels on the waste dumps, the colored lights and the large grey tent. The sun had set.

"Oh yes," Lewis said.

Beyond the circus those old houses with the fallen roofs, beyond the old houses the arid plain, beyond the plain the mountains. The smoke from the chimneys was pulled up straight in lines. A brown city tonight with dust roads between sienna blocks; a brown city bounded by hills.

"Every eight weeks they come," said Slattery. "Cheap clowns and a grey tent . . . a German ringmaster with an iron hand like Jannings. It's the Middle Ages. He's the czar . . . they never leave their tents. Looks like Emil Jannings."

"Oh yes."

"Arthur," said Slattery levelly, "what I meant about your cousin was this. You've gotta get somebody who don't like you; somebody who'll seduce her, somebody who's mean."

Lewis turned.

"If you really wanted it you'd get some kid and pay him. Set it up, make your choice, and do it right."

"Set it up?"

"Yes."

"How?"

"You know the ways!"

"I do?"

"You could figure it. He'd meet you afterward and give you an account."

Lewis took a step forward.

"Do you know anyone like this?"

"They're never hard to find," said Slattery. "Dirt is never hard to find."

"Well . . ."

"Do you want to go lookin'?"

"You mean, tonight?"

"Let me know if you really make up your mind."

Again they drank *sol y sombra;* again they drank *anís* and cognac. Around them were a hundred photographs of Manolete being gored.

"Nothing available but a veterinarian," said Slattery, "so they stitched him up like a horse."

"I was right to hit that woman."

"Do ya wanna go to a cockfight?"

"A cockfight?"

"Sunday morning. Your dick against my dick."

"I'm sure you'd win," said Lewis. "Yes, I'll come. I've never been to a cockfight."

"We'll need your conveyance. We'll need your convertible."

"Here's to us," said Lewis, raising his glass. "Yes, we'll go in the Alvis."

They drank to each other.

"A cockfight, Sunday morning. We'll go in your Alvis. I've never been to a cockfight."

A Trappist drank back a half-pint of wine behind them.

"I'm gonna turn to clay."

116

"Clay?"

"I could make you a dildo, Arthur."

"Oh shut up," Lewis said.

Slattery reached for his pocket, felt in his pocket and pulled out a crumpled paper, pulled the paper out and straightened it on the marble table top.

"I composed this while you were sleeping. After all these years I finally got it right. . . . Read it," Slattery said. "At last I've got it right."

Lewis took out his spectacles, smoothed the paper, held it up to the light.

It was a telegraph form.

It was a telegraph form addressed to Lawrence B. J. Slattery, seven hundred and sixteen Kennedy Boulevard, Boston, Massachusetts. The message read: Dear Father, Nine-eight-nine Generalísimo, Madrid. September the twentieth. Last Friday I died in my apartment. Your loving son, Patrick.

Lewis read it again.

"What is this?"

"It's my message. It's my testament. My poem."

"Your what?"

"I want to see if he'll come," said Slattery. "To my funeral."

Lewis took off his spectacles and stared.

"Are you joking?"

"Of course not. It's my poem. Will he come to my funeral? Can't send it while Mother's alive, of course."

"Thank God for that," said Lewis sarcastically.

"One day I'll send it," said Slattery. "One day I'll send it now I've got it right. I'll sign your name and send it when Mother's dead."

"You must be joking."

"I'll put 'He died in his apartment, signed A. Lewis.' "

"I think," said Lewis slowly, "that's the unkindest thing I've ever heard of. You have no right to do this. It's absolutely monstrous."

"Let me tell you about my father. I'll sign it Major Lewis."

"I don't want to hear about your father," said Lewis, "any

117

more than you want to hear about my wife. It's cruel and it is sick."

Lewis tore up the telegram and threw it onto the ground.

Lewis thought for a moment that Slattery would strike him.

Then Slattery raised his glass.

"Here's to us," said Slattery.

But before Lewis could respond Slattery tipped back his chair and stood up.

"Now let's get round to your place."

"What?"

"I don't believe there's such things as an innocent. That cousin of yours is a prick."

"You know nothing about him."

"Take me to her."

"What?"

"I'm gonna ask her a question. There's no innocents. Not in this world there ain't."

Lewis too stood up.

"I'm gonna meet your wife and ask her a question."

"You're not."

"I'm gonna knock at her door and pull her out."

"Oh no you aren't!"

"I'm gonna take her to my bedroom and lay her myself. I'll Jean her, all right."

"Sit down and be quiet," said Lewis.

"I'll give you a report. You can stand on the balcony."

"Stop it."

"You can hide in a wardrobe, you can crouch in a closet."

"Will you stop it!"

Grasping the edge of the table, leaning toward Lewis, Slattery said savagely: "I'll do it gently. I'll wine her and dine her. I'll feel her up. I'll give her a cognac. I'll give her an *anís*. My great big finger will move in circles. I'll go into a store and I'll buy me a book. I'll make me an entry with all of her details. I'll go into a store for a tape recorder. I'll measure her hole. I'll put it in my pocket and you'll have it on wheels. All through the winter evenin's you can plug it in and play it back. All her ecstasies, all her

118

screamin's. All her protests, all her endearments. All her movements and all her moans. So call me a taxi, Major."

Since they were foreigners the Spaniards did not intervene.

"I'll do it subtle, Arty. I won't tell her you sent me. I'll take me a syringe and I'll shove it up her ass. I'll take me a plunger of Nembutal. No, I won't tell her you sent me, Arty, I'll come up behind her and say I'm a friend. I'll tell her I'm bleedin' and we'll make us a movie. We'll open our wounds. We'll go into the park with a bottle of *vino,* lay right down and fuck by the fountains."

"For the last time . . ."

"I'll take her to Paris, I'll take her to the Metropole. I'll send you a cable with all our positions. I'll have her in the Vatican. I'll lay her on the altars. I'll let her out, but not on Sundays. Sundays I need her. Sundays I'll put her on top of me, Arty, Sundays I lower her by rope and I spin her like a top."

Lewis hit Slattery across the face with all his strength.

Balancing himself more squarely upon his feet, unmoved, Slattery continued: "I don't know how I'll do it, Arty, but tonight's the night I mean to begin."

Lewis hit Slattery again and again.

Slattery laughed.

"The Puerta de Hierro, you say, Arty?"

Slattery made for the door.

"Number forty-seven?"

Lewis did not answer. Lewis sat down.

"D'you wanna come and make the introduction?"

Lewis slumped wearily in his chair.

Then Slattery came back.

"It would be no good with a friend," said Lewis.

Slattery sat down.

"Not with someone I know. Not with a friend."

Slattery picked up his drink.

"I'll not talk about it again," said Lewis. "I'll not bother you again."

Slattery drained his glass.

"I've cut your lip."

119

"It's nothin'."

Slattery went to the bar, brought back two more brandies.

"Here's to us a second time."

They raised their glasses; they touched them.

"Don't think I won't remember my telegram," said Slattery. "Not now after all these years I finally got it right."

"What?"

"My telegram," said Slattery. "Have you forgotten that?"

7

They drove out north on the new highway with the roof down in the morning sun. At the end of it they turned off left, taking the road to Colmenar Viejo. There were sparrows in the wires above, flocks of still sheep on the great brown plain, and at the outskirts of the villages clouds of burning garbage.

"What a beautiful morning," Lewis said.

They turned off again to a side road, went over a railroad line, crossed a bridge with red ivy, bumped over dried mud between tall yellow grass.

"Second on the right, I was told," said Slattery. "What are you smilin' at?"

"Nothing."

"You ain't the Mona Lisa!"

At the ranch white doves circled, glided, and soared.

"We're to park in the yard, I was told," said Slattery. "Below the dove towers."

They entered the yard and parked with others beside a row of stables. In a corner a monkey was cuddling a puppy. There were horses, dogs, peacocks, and pheasants.

They got out of the Alvis.

The sun shone warm upon them. All around the cluck of the *palomas!* The monkey climbed up a dovehouse ladder.

"How pleasant," said Lewis.

"If you want a bet, tell our host."

"I don't think I'll bet."

A Spaniard with dark glasses approached, an immaculate Spaniard with a watch chain in his pocket.

The host bowed: they bowed.

121

"Mucho gusto," they said. "It is my pleasure," the Spaniard answered. "Follow."

When they took their seats: "A friend of a friend," muttered the grinning Slattery.

"I was impressed," answered Lewis.

So the ring was made, the English cocks were thrown at each other, and the silent fight began on the dust and the ashes.

Huge bottles of *vino* passed from hand to hand.

Nobody spoke.

The birds slid back, skidded, darted, sprang up, ran and leapt. The blood began to drop from the gashes in their necks.

Now their supporters shouted and their backers cried out different odds. There were no women; some of the men were laughing.

Slattery averted his eyes, but Lewis watched.

When the real fight began, when the preliminaries were over and one of the cocks had lost an eye, Slattery got out of his seat and left the yard, but Lewis watched that bleeding throat laid open, heard that crow of triumph, saw that conquering strut.

After the little crowd had gone Lewis sat on a sack of grain until Slattery came back. The dead cock lay beside him on an empty wine flask. A brown little girl with her hair in rollers brought him some bread and some olives. The monkey came down the ladder and cuddled the puppy again. Lewis wished he had some sugar for the monkey. Lewis sat there eating the olives with a curious smile come over his face—sat there smiling in that hot sun with the smell of the blood and the smell of the horses, the peacocks and the platinum pheasants back in the yard, and the white *palomas* circling above.

"Where'd you get to?"

"Olive groves. Grasshoppers rose from my feet in clouds."

"Couldn't watch it, eh?"

"No. You liked it?"

"Not exactly. Not exactly . . . though it didn't bother me. It's just that once I begin something I like to see it out."

Lewis laughed.

The waiter came to their table in brown corduroys and a vest.

"Just a jug," said Slattery. "A pretty old jug of wine."

Thick dark ivy hung around them on piers.

"Did you thank the host?"

"Of course I did. This tablecloth is beautifully darned."

On the plain before them flocks of black goats were mingling with the sheep.

Lewis laughed.

The waiter brought the wine.

"You see that line of lumpy white cloud," said Lewis. "There is blue above and blue below."

"What's the matter, Arthur?"

"You were wrong about my cousin," said Lewis, and laughed hysterically. "You were wrong and you were right."

Slattery took his wineglass, leaned back in the straw chair under the vines and the trellis, out of the burning sun.

"When did we meet last?" asked Lewis. "When was that day you told me if I really meant it to make my choice and set it up and do it right?"

"A Monday."

"When did I hit you?"

"A Monday."

"Yes, well, I thought about it all Tuesday and I decided that I did . . . I did really mean it. That all this . . . couldn't go on . . . in the long run it was necessary. True love must be generous . . . well, I won't go into all that: I know it upsets you." Again Lewis laughed.

"So I said to my cousin . . . you know . . . my cousin, who isn't nearly as nice as you thought, by the way . . . he's rather like my brother really . . . very go-ahead . . . and his accent that's sort of classless now . . . he's working for a very good firm, you see . . . he's moved into export. Well, Vernon's

123

very good at tennis . . . so's Jean . . . you'd be surprised
. . . hits to a very good length, runs for everything. I can't
beat her always, you know. I win the first set and then she out-
stays me. Anyway I arranged a singles with Vernon on Wednesday morning at the club . . . I summoned all my old resources."

"Whatever's the matter?" asked Slattery.

"I went to the net a lot . . . lobbed a lot very high into the
sun, I served with great determination. To cut a long story short
. . . I beat him three nil. In fact I gave him a damned good
thrashing. I put him right down . . . he was crestfallen. He
took it very badly. He was humiliated. Wasn't expecting it at all.
So we had a little drive after the showers. I didn't say anything in
the showers, and then I put it to him. I mean I thought out
everything you'd said . . . all its implications. I considered all
the points and what I said to Vernon was this: I said, 'Look,
Vernon, I'm having an affair, you know . . . woman of forty
at the Embassy, woman nearer my own age, on the plump side,
big bust.' I said, 'Vernon, I like them like that. Well, it's bloody
well not fair on Jean,' I said. 'I mean this friend of mine's awfully
passionate. And so is Jean. So is Jean, you see! Knows all the
tricks. Well,' I said, 'Vernon, at my age I bloody well can't
manage the two of them. This woman at the Embassy,' I said,
'well, it's only a temporary thing, she's going back to England
with her husband soon . . . about the same time as you are,
Vernon, so this is a sort of last desperate thing, you see, for her.
For Amy. I mean I know you like Jean, Vernon,' I said. 'In the
afternoons when I'm out, couldn't you get her into the old bed
with you?'

" 'Ah,' he said. 'So that's where you keep going, Uncle.'

" 'Yes,' I said. 'That's it. That's where I keep going . . . the
Embassy.'

"Vernon was quiet for a bit, then he seemed to get awfully
excited.

" 'You won't come bursting in on us?' he asked.

" 'What do you take me for,' I said. 'A photographer?'

124

" 'Supposing she doesn't want it?' he asked.

" 'Listen, Vernon,' I said, 'have a bloody good bottle of wine after lunch and start kissing her and tell her you adore her and see what bloody well happens.' "

"You were inspired," said Slattery sadly.

"I was overcome," said Lewis. " 'Don't take no for an answer, Vernon,' I said. 'Don't mention me. Say nothing but nice things about me. If she tells you I'm having an affair myself,' I said, 'don't comment. You get right in there, boy, and be physical,' I said. 'Put on a record, get some champagne and dance with her,' I said. 'She adores champagne. Probably best in the living room,' I said. 'On those rugs. Put on some Nancy Sinatra.' I remembered what you said, you see."

Lewis paused. Lewis looked out at the plain. Lewis hadn't touched his wine.

"For all I say of Vernon, you see, I like him . . . I like him but I don't know him."

The flocks of sheep and goats mingled between pylons.

"What happened?" asked Slattery. "What did that lyin' Vernon tell you?"

"She's left me," said Lewis.

Lewis began to weep.

"Oh he succeeded," Lewis said after a while, putting on his sunglasses. "Vernon succeeded. He gave me a thorough report. He said she was passive. He said it wasn't a success. He said he could hardly do it with her but thanks to the champagne he got through. 'Arthur's put you up to this, hasn't he?' she said. 'All right, fuck me. I don't mind,' Jean said, 'if that's what Arthur wants.' 'She didn't have an orgasm,' Vernon said. 'Tomorrow,' she said, 'if you're going to do it again, bring me some flowers or something, will you?' He didn't tell me about it that night. I wasn't in. I was drinking with you, I believe. That would be Wednesday night. Thursday afternoon he tried again. He did take her flowers. But it wasn't much better. Friday she'd gone. Friday she left."

"Not with Vernon."

"Oh no, not with Vernon."

Lewis looked over the plain at the mass of white cloud on the sierra.

"Vernon didn't know where she'd gone either. There was no note; she just took a few things in a suitcase. A few intimate things. She left her wedding ring. Didn't take any money. She just left the house. Just cleared out."

"Do you know where she is now?"

"Yes, I found out from a friend of hers. A girl friend. Well, not where, of course. Pauline wouldn't tell me that. But I found out who with, and what, and so forth. I got the essential facts.

"She's gone off with an American. A sort of mutual acquaintance. He's left his wife and they've gone together. He has money, I believe." Lewis paused. "He's a man of my own age," said Lewis. "A man of our age."

"I knew it wouldn't be Vernon," said Slattery.

They watched the moving men for a while together, then went out with their drinks to the pool. The willow leaves were still drowning in the water, Kleenex still floated on patches of suntan oil.

Lewis went to a corner, prized up a manhole, turned a wheel, let the green water empty.

"To think that I strove for true love," said Lewis. "This garden's going to ruin."

The ants on the concrete ran over his brogues, the willow leaves rustled behind him.

"To think that."

"Have you heard?"

"I shall give the divorce. It will be done discreetly. I shall pay all the costs, naturally."

"Where you gonna live?"

"I don't know," said Lewis.

Black butterflies flew over the hedge—on the other side old hens were clucking.

"I shall stay in Spain."

"You will?"

126

"Where else?"

Turning on one of the long black hoses, Lewis began to water the lawn.

"D'you wanna move in with me while you figure it out?"

Eyes averted, studiously hosing, Lewis answered: "I don't want to impose."

"There's no imposin'. I got room."

"Well, if I could while I . . ."

"Sort things out."

"Yes."

"You're welcome."

"That's very charming of you," said Lewis. Lewis turned off the hose, joined Slattery at the table in the rickety deck chair, picked up his drink, sat down.

"Thank you, I accept," said Lewis. "Just till I sort things out."

"You've gotta have somewhere warm for the winter," said Slattery. "We all need that."

A pine tree was drying up. A dead bird had fallen. In the center of the pool a butterfly drowned.

"Perhaps it would have been better if it had been you," said Lewis. "Perhaps it would have been better, after all, with a friend."

8

Once again snow came to the central point of Iberia, to the capital of Spain: the north wind brought it from the tops of the Guadarrama over the storks in the chimneys of the Escorial. It fell and it covered the city: the empty swimming pools, the slums, the workers' hospitals, the guarded estates, the *cervecerías, the horchaterías,* and the cafés. It closed the *aeropuerto.* It closed the Estación del Norte. It blew in the prison windows. The snow froze the pipes. Apart from emergency services electricity was cut. The town was lit with candles, siesta was slept with coats on. The university students refrained from rioting; the Cortes did not meet.

But in Slattery's building the two of them were warm: they never went out except to shop. Lewis would buy the liquor and Slattery the food.

"Do you think we should learn to ski this winter?" asked Lewis in the kitchen while Slattery cooked the supper. "Once the sun comes out. I know a couple of chaps we could borrow some boots from. We could go up to Navacerrada in the Alvis. I was always going to go up there with Jean. I was always going to get up there but we never made it."

"No."

"I'll take you up there one day for the ride. Get the snow chains out. Haven't been up the old place in the winter. We always meant to but never made it."

"Pass me the salt, will ya?"

"In the winter in Madrid the fans are always idle. Have you noticed that?"

"I have."

"I was wondering if we ought to get a television."

128

"Over my dead body," Slattery said.

"Not for the bullfights?"

"Not for nothin'. Pass me the garlic, will ya?"

"Is it my fault you can't work?"

"No."

"Would it be better if I left?"

"It's nothing to do with you."

"If you had another painter share the place that might help. If you have a young painter around wouldn't that cheer you up?"

"It wouldn't. Try this."

Lewis took the spoon and tasted.

"Marvelous," Lewis said.

"Sit yourself down."

Lewis did so.

"Then let me at least pay half the rent."

"We're my father's guests," said Slattery, opening a bottle. "We're the remittance men, we're the exiles, kid. You talk too much. I ought to get my mother over here. I ought to but I can't. I don't know why she hasn't written."

"Perhaps she's got the flu," said Lewis. "I believe there's an awful lot of it around."

"I think I ought to warn ya. I ought to warn ya I get depressions. I get depressions like a woman. And when I get 'em I go nutty, so watch out."

"Yes."

"If I could get my mother over here we'd look after her."

"We could look after her and take her out," said Lewis.

"I've bought a book on this skiing for when the weather turns," Lewis said. "I hate instructors."

"I wrote my mother. I asked her to come."

"You see we could go up there and begin very gently. Just to get some air, really."

"I wrote her. I should hear any day now."

Outside the windows a wet grey mist covered the plain and the mountains.

"Why can't I paint?" asked Slattery.

. . . . .

129

The mountains and the pine forests drew nearer. The lower slopes were dull; above, the peaks were silver.

"I was hoping to hear from Jean, but she didn't answer."

"I can't think why I haven't heard," said Slattery.

"I told her if anything . . . anything went wrong . . . she could always . . ."

"Count on you."

"Yes."

"I think I'll write to my sister about it," said Slattery.

They passed a workers' rest home and climbed higher. Above, the peaks were flashing.

"I'll have to be putting the chains on."

"I'll write to my sister," said Slattery. "I figure my father's interceptin' the mail."

"This American fellow's wife won't give her husband a divorce," Lewis said. "She seems to be resolute about that."

They had entered the pine woods and the mountains. The sun and the snow were dazzling.

"If I hadn't had to fix those skis up there we could have had the roof down."

The car began to skid.

"We must stop and put our snow chains on," said Lewis.

They came out of the bar of the Arias Hotel, blinked, rubbed their eyes, and stared at the gleaming valley. They looked all the way to their city.

"You serious about this?" asked Slattery, turning up the hill.

The skiers on the slopes above darted and twisted like tadpoles.

"Oh, that's too steep for us, that bit," said Lewis. "We're on the nursery."

Lewis started to undo the borrowed skis from the roof of the Alvis.

"Best put our boots on here, I think, while our hands are warm. That's what they say . . . put your boots on in the warm. They say that in the book."

"Yeah, let's put 'em on in the warm," said Slattery. Slattery took his boots, and went back to the bar.

130

. . . . .

"This is ridiculous," said Slattery. "These boots are killin' me."

"Bound to at first."

The snow they stood in was soft and damp.

"I got different bones in my feet. The guy that wears these boots can't have no bones. I've got bones that stick out at the side."

"The first lesson is stepping around," said Lewis.

"What the hell's that?"

Slattery's breath rose into the air like steam from a boiling pot.

"You step around in small steps. You lift one end of your ski while your other end's stationary."

"I bet your end isn't stationary."

"Oh shut up. Let's try it."

"Why?"

"Because it'll be good for us," said Lewis. "That's why."

Slattery laughed.

"We've got to do something," said Lewis. "Now I'll get the book out and read it to you while you try it."

"No," said Slattery. "I'll read the book and you can try it. It was your idea to get us up here on this sierra."

"Spoilsport."

"I can't move in these boots," said Slattery. "They're killin' me, these boots. The guy's got no bones."

"Lazy bastard."

"Give me the book."

Lewis gave Slattery the book.

"All right, you read it out and I'll do it first. Then we'll do it together. Over there."

They walked between children to a flat place. The snow was firmer here.

"You know how to put 'em on?"

"I've read that bit," said Lewis.

Lewis put his skis on: gingerly stood up. His feet slid apart.

"Hand me my poles, Patrick."

131

Slattery did so.

"Okay, read to me. Page eighteen, I believe it is."

Laughing, holding the book in one hand and taking a flask out of his pocket with the other, Slattery drank and read in his imitation of Lewis's English accent: " 'There are two ways of stepping around. One is to step the ski tips around while the tails remain on the snow. The other is to keep the tips stationary and step the tails around.

" 'Let's step the tips around first.' Yeah, let's step your tits around first."

"Go on, I'm getting cold."

"Let's step your tits around first. 'Pretend you're standing on the dial of a large clock, facing the rim.' " Bursting into a shriek of obscene laughter, Slattery repeated: "Pretend you're standing on the dial of a large cock, facing the rim. Your skis move around with the hands of the cock. The fronts go round while the tails remain in the snow on the center. Starting with the tits of both skis at twelve o'cock, step the tit of the right ski to one o'cock. Step the left tit up to it. Step up your left tit."

But resolutely, seriously, sucking in his cheeks as he did so, Lewis began and continued until he had completed a circle.

" 'Now go around the dial countercockwise, starting with a step to the left,' " read Slattery, still grinning.

"Oh no! Now you'll do it with me," said Lewis. "Come on, you great ass."

So under Lewis's direction Slattery laid down the book and struggled into his skis.

"Stand up," said Lewis.

Heaving himself up on his poles, like a gorilla, Slattery did so.

"Okay!" said Lewis. "Okay, smarty. Now let's see how easy you think it is. I'll race you around."

"What?"

"Let's see who can complete the circle first."

"What?"

"You're always saying you're an athlete."

"Yeah, but you've had practice."

132

"All right, don't if you don't want to," said Lewis condescendingly. "I mean if you don't want to."

Slattery frowned.

"Who's gonna say go?" asked Slattery, putting the flask back into his pocket.

"You can."

"No. You say it. Even though you've had practice."

"Ready then?"

"Let's face each other. Let's get head-on. Let's look at each other like contestants."

"Okay."

They moved and stood opposite. They were tense. They braced themselves.

"Okay."

"Okay."

"Which way round?"

"To the left," said Lewis.

"Okay. To the left."

"Okay?"

"Okay."

There wasn't a cloud in the sky above them.

"Go," cried Lewis, and in his first effort to move quickly picked his entire right ski off the ground, stood on his left ski with it, and fell, while Slattery, who had made precisely the same mistake, stood trapped with crossed skis, glowering and heaving.

When Slattery saw that Lewis had fallen he cried out in triumph: "I've won! I've won. Anybody who falls has lost! That's the rule."

But Lewis did not answer.

"Get up, you lost!" shouted Slattery.

"I don't think I can," muttered Lewis.

"What?"

"I've hurt myself," said Lewis.

"Get up, you old idiot."

"I'm telling you I can't."

"Jesus," said Slattery. "Are ya ruptured?"

133

Slattery managed at last to uncross his skis.

"How do I get out of these?"

Lewis did not answer.

"How do I get out of these, Arthur?" shouted Slattery in a rage.

But Lewis had fainted.

When finally Slattery succeeded in undoing the bindings, getting out of his skis, and going to Lewis, he found that Lewis had broken his leg. Lewis had to be taken down to Madrid in an ambulance to the British and American hospital.

Sunday.

My dear Art,

I'm sorry I haven't come to see you but I can't take hospitals. I never could. It's the smell and those white uniforms that get me. Also the needles. I'm having your room spring-cleaned. I told the maid once but she didn't do it right so I'm having her do it again. I said "spring-clean" not flick it with a dustrag. That's what I said to her.

I got your car down all right. It's in the garage across the street. I returned the bloody skis but I kept the book for you.

No trouble will come to your car because I'm not allowed to drive. The boy that brought it says it's okay.

Some clothes of your wife's turned up here—the new owner found them in a closet so I've stored 'em. Should I throw 'em out or what? Just hats and a coat and things.

I can't paint so I'm going to try clay. I might do a self-head. What about that for a laugh! They could put it in the ape house.

I could do you when you get out. They could put *that* with the other ski champions, and gold medalists.

I haven't heard from my sister so I'm writing to my father direct.

If that don't work I'll put out a police call for her. I mean what's going on.

What's going on, eh Art?

I heard Francy married an Englishman. You guys are suckers for punishment. I hear he's a mechanic in Marbella. Sports cars!

Still maybe I did her some good after all. It wasn't all bad.

134

I had a couple of my "depressions" but luckily no one came to too much harm. One was on St. Patrick's night! I think. Or was that last year.

Try and lay one of the nurses.

I'll be seein' you when you get out,

Patrick

P.S.   If not one of the nurses one of the nuns that keep coming in and out of that joint.

Sunday again. With the bells ringing.

Dear Art,

Spring is here. I'll bet your dick is rising out of its plaster. Thank you for your letter. I'm not surprised to hear your bones are brittle. Thank Christ you're coming out.

If I could get enough hooch inside me I would try and get in there. It's just those white uniforms and that smell, you understand. Also they have iron bars over the windows.

I've had that bloody maid do your room again. This time I stood over her while she got down on her hands and knees. I think she thought I was going to ram her but I denied her that privilege.

I'm getting on with my head. It's getting to become a thing of true monstrosity. I've moved the pictures out and put mirrors in and now I can compare us from all sides. At the moment I'm still winning but the monstrosity on the pedestal is gaining on me. They're Victorian mirrors—you'll like them.

For Christ's sake get out of there. If you'd had children I guess it would've been different. But who knows.

It isn't the same drinking without you.

Patrick

P.S.   I'll do what you say with your wife's clothes as soon as I get round to it. I hate that bastard marble hall of a post office as you know. If I go in there I might send that telegram of mine by mistake. I haven't heard from my father.

P.P.S.   I'll be waiting outside the iron gates on Thursday with a brass band playing "God Save the Queen" and Francy's mother naked in the Alvis.

P.P.P.S.   I have just remembered that on no account are you to let them plaster your dick again. If you want your dick to be immortalized, far better that the hand of a master should mold it in clay. I will do this for a small charge. I'd send your dick some flowers while he's waiting but I don't want anyone in there to think he's a fairy.

P.P.P.P.S.   I am sorry to have to ask your dick for a charge but we must never forget that I am a professional. We must never forget that!

Lewis was awakened from a dream in which Jean returned to him, kissed him, and begged for forgiveness, by the door of his hospital room bursting open and the light going on.

Somewhere there was shouting and running footsteps.

"Ah, there you are, my dear!"

Slattery stood in the doorway grinning.

Lewis lay staring up at him.

Slattery stood in the doorway swaying.

Slattery wore a woman's green hat on his head—a hat with a veil—and the end of the veil half-caught in his grey mustache.

Lewis reached for his glasses. He had seen that the hat was his wife's.

"I come from the post office, I come from the *palacio de comunicaciones,* but they threw me out. I tried to climb their tower but I couldn't make it. They don't accept obscene mail through the post. They wouldn't take this."

Slattery drew an old suspender belt from his trouser pocket and waved it about in the air.

"They wouldn't send this through the *comunicaciones.* They said it's dirty. She's a very clean woman, *I* said. I know that. Arthur told me."

Adjusting his glasses, Lewis sat up in the bed, best as he could.

"You're terribly drunk."

"Drunk!"

A film dropped over Slattery's eyes. He advanced.

"Watch it."

136

In the corridors there was shouting. A man could be heard running. Now nurses appeared behind Slattery and they too shouted and waved their arms.

Laughing at these nurses, shouting "Just come to see my friend," Slattery slammed the door shut, wedged a chair beneath its handle.

Slattery shouted again: "Just come to see my friend."

Slattery piled the rest of the furniture in the room over and round and under the chair, singing in a high-pitched English falsetto: " 'If you were the only girl in the world, and I was the only boy.' "

Slattery went over to Lewis's wardrobe, took that up, and wedged it between Lewis's bed and the pile of furniture around the door.

Seeing the suspender belt on the floor, Slattery seized it again, tied it about his neck, cleared the veil from his mustache, advanced toward Lewis's bed, and changing from the high falsetto to a voice level approximating Lewis's own, sucked in his cheeks to sing in a sort of Julie Andrews *My Fair Lady* Cockney:

"I'm very fond of my old wife,
Are you? Yes, I am!"

Something telling him that if he offended his friend further, or said again the wrong thing, he would be in danger, Lewis closed his eyes and sighed as if he were sitting there in that hospital bed in considerable pain.

"You're acting, are ya, you faggot! Let's see what that leg's like."

Giving Lewis what he considered to be a playful dig in the ribs but which Lewis felt to be a sledgehammer blow to the body, Slattery pulled Lewis's blankets off.

"Got dick trussed up, I see."

Slattery banged the plaster on the leg with his fist.

"The bastards are doin' this deliberate."

"It's coming off tomorrow," said Lewis.

"They're doin' this deliberate. They ain't told ya you got gangrene in there. They're takin' their revenge for Gibraltar."

137

"Coming off tomorrow," said Lewis gently.

"What have you got in there?" demanded Slattery, banging the plaster again. "What have you got in there? Nettles? Broken glass?"

Someone began to bang on the door of the room.

"Aw, piss off," shouted Slattery, wheeling around toward it and clenching both massive battered fists. "Piss off, you noisy Spaniards. Piss off, you oyga diggas."

"Patrick, for God's sake," implored Lewis. "They'll jail you."

"*Abajo con España.*"

"Oh God," muttered Lewis. "Oh please God, calm him."

Lewis saw that Slattery's hip pocket was bulging with pesetas.

Desperate now to change Slattery's turn of abuse, fearful that they would find themselves before a Spanish court and both be deported or worse, Lewis cried out: "*Viva Franco. Viva España.*" Lewis lunged violently at Slattery's hip pocket, reaching for Slattery's pesetas, seeking to distract him.

"*Viva Franco. Viva España.*"

But Lewis missed. And groaned when the plaster tore his skin at the upper part of his leg.

Seeing Lewis's plight, laughing at Lewis's intention, but knowing the reason for it, Slattery allowed a look of cunning to flash over his face, a look of wariness, a look of practice, and he too began to shout at the top of his voice: "*Viva Franco. Viva España. Viva Franco. Arriba España.*"

Outside the shouting and banging continued.

Hearing the new cries from Slattery, Lewis lay still in relief.

Gazing at Lewis, giggling now, Slattery pulled a pair of women's nylon panties out of his trouser pocket, stepped into them, and began to pull them over his trouser legs.

"Mother's in the madhouse.
Mother's in the madhouse."

"What?" asked Lewis.

Tugging the panties around his behind, Slattery went on crooning:

138

"Mother's in the nuthouse.
Mother's in the snake pit."

"What?" asked Lewis in horror.

"They put her away," said Slattery. "They had my mother committed. I went down there to the post office with your wife's panties and my telegram but they wouldn't take it."

Dancing up and down, kicking out his legs like a chorus girl, thumbs in the pink panties around his trousers, Slattery sang:

"Any old iron
Any old iron
Any any any old iron."

Slattery stopped. "Yeah, they put her away," he announced. "They put her in the loony bin."

"How long ago?"

"I'll be up your flue
In a minute or two."

"But is it just for treatment?"

"Father drove her nutty!
Father drove her nutty!
Father fucked her nutty!"

Appalled at the nature of the smile on Slattery's jigging, mumbling face, Lewis screamed: "Pull yourself together!"

"Nobody told me
Nobody told me
Maybe I could've helped her
Maybe I could've helped her,"

sang Slattery, jigging and shuffling as before.

"If you don't pull yourself together," shouted Lewis, "you'll be right in there with her."

"That's a good idea," said Slattery, abruptly stopping his dance and opening his eyes wide. "I'll break in there and get her out."

139

"You're a bloody fool."

"He should've told me," said Slattery in a low, almost sober tone.

"Maybe he wanted to spare you," said Lewis. "Maybe he wanted to spare you."

"The bastard drove her to it, he committed her deliberately," said Slattery as soberly as before. The eyes misting over again, reverting, he picked up Lewis's crutch and sang like an Irish tenor: "Does your mother come from Ireland?"

There was silence outside the door: authoritative footsteps approached. Lewis heard them but Slattery took no notice. Slattery started banging on the floor with Lewis's crutch, crooning like a Negro blues singer. "Hey you down there, you down there, come up and join me, baby, out of the grave."

"Policía. Policía."

Slattery wheeled on the door, pointed Lewis's crutch at it, let off a burst of sound like a machine gun firing.

"For God's sake," cried Lewis, "keep quiet or you'll get shot."

"Está bien. Está bien," shouted Lewis. *"Mi amigo. Amigo. Espere, por favor. Espere, por favor.*

"Patrick," said Lewis.

Their eyes met.

"Patrick," said Lewis, "it's the police. Now don't mess them about or you're going to get beaten up. Perhaps you'll get shot."

"Wouldn't let me send my telegram," said Slattery. "He drove her to it."

"Take those knickers and that hat off."

"What?"

"They don't like to see you in knickers," said Lewis. "The police don't. Remember that?"

"I'll send it somehow."

"Take those knickers off, and the hat, and the suspender belt, and bring them here."

Slattery laughed.

"Want 'em to wrap around your prick? Do you?"

"Do what I say or they'll beat the hell out of you."

140

"Policía. Policía."

Slattery shivered.

"Espere, por favor," called Lewis.

Slattery took off the hat, untied the suspender belt, pulled off the panties.

"Bring them here," said Lewis.

Slattery did so.

"Put my blanket back on me," said Lewis.

Slattery did so.

Lewis put Jean's old garments under his blanket.

Slattery swayed.

"Viva España," called Slattery.

"Okay, open up," said Lewis. "Whatever you do, go quietly. Don't do any more punching or kicking. Whatever they say to you, keep quiet. If you get punched or kicked, don't kick back."

"I've been around."

"Do what I tell you, for God's sake."

"Yes. I'll do that."

"I'll be waiting for you."

"The porter has a key."

"What?"

"The porter has a key to the apartment."

"Thank you. Good."

Slattery stood up straight—he might never have had a drink in his life.

"The trouble with those places," Slattery said slowly, "the trouble with those places is they turn ya nuts even if you aren't. When you go in."

Slattery went to the door, began to remove the furniture.

"I won't answer back," said Slattery. "I'm gonna climb into the van and sit quietly because somehow or other I've got to get Mother out."

Slattery removed the rest of the furniture, opened the door, put his hands on his head, called: *"España, me gusta mucho."* And went.

Lewis's leg was throbbing.

After they had made up Lewis's bed, tidied his room, sympa-

141

thized with him, put out his light, and left him alone in the dark again, Lewis wept. But whether it was for himself, or Jean, or Slattery's mother, or Slattery, or all of them, Lewis could not have said.

9

It was a beautiful afternoon at the end of spring, with blossom everywhere, when Lewis met Slattery in the Alvis at the gates of the jail.

"You look thinner but well."

"I got off light."

"They treated you decently?"

"Second time in they've always got somethin' against you. One more, and I'm deported."

"Really."

"I can't go to Italy. I can't go to Rome. The Pope don't like me. One more time and I'm deported from *España!*"

"Really."

"They don't allow me in France."

"I didn't know that!"

Slattery sniffed at the smell on the orange trees.

"You look thinner yourself."

"Very fit. Very fit. But the damned leg still pains me. We could always go to India, I suppose."

"And get poisoned."

Slattery went to the orange tree, took blossom in his hand, and crushed it. Slattery rubbed the crushed blossom on his face.

"We could opt out totally," said Slattery. "We could always totally opt out."

Lewis got into the Alvis and started it; the Alvis was polished and gleaming.

"I have some letters for you in my pocket."

"I know you have," said Slattery. "They're answers to certain queries . . . one's from my father and the other's from the Institute."

Slattery left the orange tree and came to the Alvis.

"D'you want them now?"

"Later. Let's breathe the air a while."

Slattery went round the back of the Alvis and got in.

"Thank you for all your assistance," said Slattery.

Slowly they drove into Madrid. The road was being widened on both sides.

"I remember when one could do this journey in a quarter of the time," said Lewis. "I do begin to wonder where else we might live."

They choked in the fumes from the diesels. They gazed at the urbanizations.

"Jean's friend got his divorce after all, so they'll marry," Lewis said.

Jet trails hung low in the blue above them. The air was full of noise and dust.

"Apparently she's pregnant . . . that's why the chap's wife gave it to him," Lewis said.

Slattery seemed preoccupied and did not comment.

They passed down a long avenue of budding trees behind the roaring trucks. They stopped. They started. They stopped. To their left a large Madonna hung down on a long black chain. Slattery looked at it.

"Hi, Mother," Slattery said.

Barefoot boys played games on the steps of the church—black-veiled penitent women kept climbing up. There were piles of rubble on the pavement, and a couple of rats wandered across.

"So give me the letters."

Lewis took the letters out of his pocket and handed them over.

"Which shall I read first?"

"Your father's."

Slattery put down his father's letter on the table before him, took up a knife, and slit open the letter from the Institute.

In this *mesón* almost everything was white or black—only the brasswork broke up the pattern: the lamps, the pans, the

144

breeches of the flintlocks hanging on the walls and over the hearth.

" 'I will admit that her position is deteriorating somewhat,' " read Slattery.

Lewis put down his coffee spoon, leaned forward in his chair.

Slattery read again: " 'To be frank I will admit that her position is deteriorating somewhat. Her periods of depression are more severe and on the increase. There are still days, however, when your mother is cheerful and tells me that she is her old self. I cannot pretend to you that the surroundings and the sight of some of the other patients do not affect her. However, without properly trained and devoted care twenty-four hours of the day I would not dream of recommending her release from here. Many conditions would have to be fulfilled, or rather seem able to be fulfilled, if I am to take the matter up with the various persons concerned. Your father, of course . . .' "

Slattery stopped reading the letter.

"My father put her in there," said Slattery. "I told you that."

"Go on."

Slattery read: " 'Your father, of course, would have to be consulted first. Naturally I have not said anything about your letter to your mother. Obviously it would not do to excite her in any way at this point. You will appreciate that when a person is in your mother's condition it can be quite disastrous to raise their hopes and then have to tell them those hopes cannot be fulfilled.' "

Slattery stopped reading.

"He pays to keep me out of the country; he pays to keep her in a snake pit."

"What else does the doctor say?"

Slattery read: " 'To satisfy my curiosity about her relationship with yourself without in any way raising suspicions in her that I might now have a special interest, I have encouraged her to talk about her children—which she likes to do in any case. I must tell you when she speaks of you her face particularly brightens. She speaks often of your school days, how you looked,

145

and what a fine runner you were. How tall and how strong. She told me she went to see you run in a race at Madison Square Garden and you won. She was so proud. One day, when at first I thought her to be extremely low, she turned to me and said smilingly: "I know one shouldn't have favorites . . . I know that now . . . but of all my children, Patrick . . . Patrick was the one I specially loved." ' "

Slattery's voice trailed away. He put down the letter on the table.

"Shall I . . . shall I read it?" asked Lewis tentatively, after a pause.

"Yeah, you read it . . . try to make out the salient points."

Lewis read the letter, ordered another coffee, read the letter again.

"You see, she agreed to be committed. She agreed to go in there."

"He drove her to it."

"Her own doctor persuaded her, I would think."

"He's *his* doctor. You don't know these American police chiefs."

"But Patrick," said Lewis, "now listen to me very carefully. How old's your father?"

"What's that got to do with it?"

"How old is your father?" repeated Lewis.

"Eighty. Eighty-two."

"It might be very difficult for him at that age. Perhaps your father just can't cope. And I suppose . . . he'd have to have a full-time trained nurse . . . maybe two of them. Two nurses! I imagine that would be very expensive for him, particularly in the United States."

"He made enough from his thievin'. What do ya think I get? That's why I get drunk every month. I get blood money."

"Be reasonable. It may be too much of a strain on your father. Your father might be ill too. He's a very old man. Let's face it, if she's not looked after properly your mother could kill herself at any moment."

146

After an explosive pause Slattery unclenched his fists and muttered: "I know that. I know that."

"The whole thing is," said Lewis, holding up the letter, "if you're going to satisfy all these requirements . . . the doctors, herself, the financial problems . . . your father . . . you're going to have to go there. You're going to have to go there and get her out."

There was another pause.

"You haven't got a hope in hell of persuading them if you don't *go* there."

"Give me one of your cigars."

Lewis did so. Slattery leaned across the table. A waiter was too quick for Lewis and the waiter lit Slattery's cigar.

"Muchas gracias."

Slattery drew deep.

"How could you do that? How could you *possibly* go there?"

Laying down the cigar upon the ash tray Slattery answered: "She's not in New York State. She's not in Massachusetts. They took her across the river and put her in Vermont."

Slattery smiled with joy as if at this very moment he'd got his mother out.

"So?"

"I didn't commit any of my misdemeanors in Vermont."

"Ah," said Lewis. "Ah, those funny American state laws."

"I need a good lawyer. I need that Louis Nizer."

"If your father stops your money . . . if your father stops your money," said Lewis slowly, "and you need . . ."

"A bit of cash."

"Yes. A bit of cash."

"You can always help out."

"Yes, well, I could."

"Don't think I won't be taking it."

"I mean you could have the money from the sale of my house," said Lewis.

The smell of the olives—the smell of the sweat and cooking in the street.

147

"Television in there. I'm not goin' in there."

"I like the plates."

"Plates?"

"Every plate in there's got a different face."

"Yeah, but look at the barman, he's wearin' a wig. There's only men in there, you see that, don't you?"

"Aren't the fish pretty," said Lewis. "Scarlet, gold, orange and red."

Tomatoes, bay leaves, dirty napkins, peppers, onions, cheese, and eggs.

"So we'll get that letter off in the morning," said Lewis.

"We'll make your appointment and off we'll go to the States."

"*You* can deal with the lawyers."

"I will."

"I think you'll do best with the lawyers."

"Yes."

"I think you'll do great with the lawyers," said Slattery. "You in your glasses and your English suits."

Here the walls were all yellow—like parchment the faded bulls, the faded matadors.

"Did ya go in my room?"

"What room?"

"Did you see the unfinished monster?"

"No."

"Why not?"

"I didn't like to. I don't go into people's rooms without being asked," Lewis said.

They felt drunk with achievement and yet they'd only drunk beers. On the teak benches beside them the old men were tired.

"The guy who did that ceiling was killed in the Civil War."

Lewis saw wood-carved figures on the ceiling where Slattery pointed—tiny gleaming figures. As if they'd been sunk in oil and shrunk like human heads, Lewis thought.

"But you could've gone into my room without askin'," Slattery said.

Outside on the sidewalk the old men sat on rickety cheap chairs with rheum in their eyes. There was a boy there who

148

served only old men. There were women with earrings like pagodas. There were women slapping their thighs and laughing. Big black-haired fat women greasy as olives.

A shoeblack took "no" for an answer, so they entered.

The barman wore a blue-green butcher's apron.

"*Mariscos* for mariners," said Lewis.

"What I intend to do," said Slattery, "what I intend to do while we're waitin' is to scrap my head and do one for Mother."

The clocks between the dead bullfighters stood with the hands at seven.

"That would be somethin' for her. I could put my *best* work into that."

"It would certainly cheer her up, I should think."

There were gas lamps with three prongs in case the neon strips went off.

"Yes, I'll do a head of my mother."

"What about your *father's* letter?" asked Lewis. "You never read that."

"Give it to me."

They got their beers and they raised their glasses. Naked the light bulbs hanging overhead.

"Who needs it," said Slattery, "on a night like this."

Slattery took hold of his father's letter, winked at Lewis, and tore the letter up.

This was the night they got drunk on a dozen Spanish beers.

10

Even in the middle of the Alcala birds were singing this morning.

We can give his mother the time of her life. We can look after her like nobody else.

Lewis was whistling. The roof was down: whenever he had to stop in the dense traffic he tapped out the tune with his fingers on the outside of the Alvis door.

They would engage Spanish nurses—English-speaking Spanish nurses—so much cheaper.

Lewis bore left to the Puerto del Sol.

When he moved in his seat to change gear he felt the plane tickets in his trouser hip pocket. Lewis accelerated, cut in on the inside, and laughed at those Spanish Séats. When Slattery got into a depression he'd simply tell the nurses and take Slattery out—take Slattery out for the night, but stick with him wherever he went. The sight of Slattery's mother might calm him—the responsibility *would* calm him. Maybe Slattery would sculpt even better than he could paint.

Lewis found the street: on one side stood those horrible buildings from the thirties—on the other grey stone with barred windows.

What would Mrs. Slattery say when the doctor told her Patrick was coming? How would she look? How would she smile? Perhaps Mrs. Slattery could still speak Spanish. Mrs. Slattery would pick it up again from her nurses. They would stay in Madrid for the springs and the autumns, and in the winters and in the summers they would go down to the south.

Whenever unhappy thoughts intruded upon him Lewis was able to throw them out.

"I am the only one . . . the only one in my family, Arthur, prepared to look after my mother. Seven kids, Arthur, and me the eldest, and the only one. Think of that. Such is life."

When Lewis saw the building he wanted—the Real Academía de Bellas Artes de San Fernando, founded in 1774 by Charles the Third, Lewis searched for a parking place, found one, and got out. The front of the building was imposing—a portico supported by two Doric columns, and the entrance guarded by two enormous paneled wooden doors. He walked toward it whistling.

Lewis went through one of the doors and found himself in a courtyard with none of the bright sunlight shining down from above. On his left stood an ancient Greek goddess; on his right, Hercules. This courtyard faced another entrance. Beyond this second entrance the main arched vaulted corridor led on to further courtyards and further balconies. Lewis crossed and proceeded. In spite of the gloom in the next courtyard Lewis went on whistling.

When he reached the building within the buildings, such was the darkness that a light shone out like a beacon through the *portero*'s glass-paned door. Lewis knocked on the door and a dwarf answered, telling him to come in. Leaving the shade, Lewis entered. The dwarf sat in a faded blue uniform. With the dwarf were a rickety table, a naked light bulb dangling from the ceiling, a small shelf with some medicine bottles, and in a tiny vase, one dying flower.

Lewis told the *portero* his business; the old dwarf nodded and pointed.

In the back a staircase led to the cellars. Urged on, Lewis went to it and descended. He wasn't whistling now because of the damp and the decay; and the sight of the other old men at the bottom.

Lewis went gingerly because of his leg; down here it was slippery. His leg had started to throb. If he had known he would have brought his walking stick.

"Can I buy some *barro,* some clay, here?" Lewis asked.

"Certainly," they said.

151

"I can buy some clay?"

"All the art students do," they said. "How much do you want?"

"Enough for a head."

"Have you transport? The clay is heavy."

"Ah."

"Clay is heavier than lead."

"Oh yes, I have transport," Lewis answered, thinking of the springs of his Alvis.

"You have transport?"

"Oh yes, I have transport," Lewis answered, thinking of his leg and the stairs and the long walk back.

There was no one here under seventy but himself.

"How much do you want?"

"Enough for a head."

"Well, that's four blocks," the old men told him, "that's four blocks, maybe five."

"Five?"

"Five blocks for a large head," they said, speaking together. "Five."

"Thirty pesetas a block," the old men said.

"I must find a boy. I must find a boy to carry it. I'll find a boy and I'll come back."

"You find a boy and we'll prepare it," the old men said.

At the corner of the Puerta Cerrada Lewis found the Cava Baja. The dirty old warehouse was green-shuttered in the dusk.

Lewis parked and entered.

There was every kind of hardware in this one big dim-lit room. On one side knives and scissor boxes to the ceiling—on the other pots and pans.

Walking to the enamelware counter Lewis was whistling again. "Two yards, thank you, Arthur," Slattery had said. Lewis could see the rolls of wire on the floor at the foot of the counter. *Tela metálica,* Slattery had said. *Tela metálica . . .* two yards for Mother's head . . . can't do her all of clay," Slattery had said.

152

This time there were four or five old men attendants—this time their overalls were red. Here all the old men ran to serve him like competitors.

"So here's to Mother," said Slattery as they sat on the floor in the wire and the clay.

"To Mother."

"And here's to us," said Lewis.

Lewis saw their happy reflections in the great mirrors, sat on his crate of beer and giggled. Lewis raised his beer to the sightless, massive, half-formed grey head in the corner, to the young woman's head emerging on top of the pedestal, to Slattery, to himself: to everyone.

Lewis wished that he too might have been an artist.

"No hard stuff . . . beers from now on," said Slattery.

"You walk right round a head and from every point of view it's different," said Lewis in joy and admiration.

"I'm doin' her young," Slattery said.

11

The sun blazed through the cracks in the window blinds.

"I know you disapprove."

"I do."

"What I mean is . . . I never used to like it in the big rings because that's a spectacle. That's very cold. I always felt quite detached . . . always longed for the bull to win. In those big rings it seemed to me to be no contest whatsoever. I wanted them to bring in a lion, or a tiger . . . or one of your American bears. I believe one of those big grizzly bears would try and get the bull by the nose . . . try and blind it. Very clever those bears, you know . . . only animal, I understand, that will backtrack itself. Or a rhinoceros. What would happen then? I must say, if I had the money . . . if I had my own amphitheater . . . I would like to fix up a few of these contests. It seemed to me in those big plazas it was no contest . . . quite unequal . . . all that bloodletting first. I mean possibly if the man had to do it all I thought . . . the man all by himself with a sword from the beginning . . . he could use the big cape, of course . . . that would be fair enough . . . as it is, the contest's unequal. That's what I thought until I went to the small rings, but then I *saw* . . . when I sat there in San Sebastián for the first time right on the *barrera* . . . on the bloody *barrera* . . . I realized how dangerous it really was. Then I saw why the man needed help. That's when *I* got involved. Especially with the *novilleros,* because half of them have no skill. And they show off. But it's their courage, you see, that gets me. Say what you like, human courage is appealing. It *is,* you know. Down there in those small rings it really is a matter of life and death. That's what excites me. Those *novilleros* are mad, you see, mad with

154

courage and fear. They're all trying to attract the critics, you see, that's the irony of it. All trying to attract the critics so they can get into the big rings. Now I'm no purist but when you see them as close as that . . . sweating with the fear of it . . . gearing themselves up . . . and then those bloody horns going by . . . and that neck . . . well, I tell you, I'm no purist but in those small rings I sweat with fear myself and if it's any good at all I jump to my feet and I shout *ole* with fervor."

"Piss off, will ya."

"The point is . . . in these small rings in that front row . . . whoever you are you must be involved. You can see just what it's like to be out there. Half the time you can reach out and touch them."

"I am trying to work."

Lewis looked at his watch.

"I sent the telegram."

"You've told me that five times."

"We get there ten thirty Wednesday morning your time. I mean Vermont time. We get to Vermont ten thirty."

"You told me that," Slattery said.

"There'll be the drive, of course. I'll work that out. I'll work that out in the plane. I've done all the packing except for the sponge bags."

"The what?"

"I haven't done the sponge bags yet. I mean I haven't packed the toothbrushes and the shaving things. All right?"

"Thank you."

"I'm rather excited, you know. I've never been to the States, of course. All my opinions of it are secondhand, you see. What about supper?"

"Supper?"

"Shall I cook it for a change?"

"I don't want any supper. I wanna work."

"You must have something to eat."

"Meet you at Mexico Lindo's at ten o'clock."

Lewis went to the door.

Slattery and the girl's head shone in all the mirrors.

"She *is* coming along well, isn't she? Beautiful!"

"For the last time," shouted Slattery, "if you don't piss off I'll hit *you* over the head with this mallet."

When Lewis came out of the studio he didn't know what to do next: it was an hour to the bullfights, an hour to the races.

He walked down the corridor muttering: "He should come with me, he needs some air."

He went to his room, turned on the air conditioner, and lay down on his bed: as soon as he did so he had to shut out his wife. He turned onto his stomach, he buried his face. "What I take as my ideal," he muttered, "is what makes for the most happiness. I was right even if I was wrong."

Lewis lay there. He took off his hat and bowed to the President. The crowd cried: "Major Lewis!" But it was only when he took the cape and walked out into the red ring that they saw he had an artificial leg. The bull charged. "My trouble is I have no resources," said Lewis, opening his eyes and closing them again. Slowly Lewis moved the cape just ahead of the bull's horns and passed the bull with no other movement but his arms. On the last pass Lewis turned his back, stopped the bull, bowed, and returned to the *callejón.* "I suppose she'll die one day," he said. The horses entered. He waved to the President: the picadors left. The *banderillas* were placed very quickly. The crowd remained standing. The sun shone and there was no wind. The bull was big, still strong, still fierce, still fast, and hooked to the right. Lewis dedicated the bull to the crowd; the crowd went mad with joy. Lewis bowed. "I do wish I believed in the life eternal," said Lewis. On the first charge the bull ran straight. Lewis put his feet together and did not move. Lewis stood exalted and thrust his waist at the horns again and again and again. With his wrists alone Lewis turned the bull around him in circles, passing the bull so close across his chest that the bull's shoulder trailed blood upon him and one of the *banderillas* struck him, and fell out at his feet on the sand. Lewis opened his eyes, looked at his watch, pushed himself up. His throat was parched, his tongue was stiff. He went to the basin and drank

156

from the tap. He looked at himself in the mirror. "Not one trick, you see," he said ironically. "A matador from another age." He left his room, went to the elevator, and descended. He got into the Alvis. Halfway down the Generalísimo he drew the bull again and wound it around him. He passed the bull with his right hand, he passed it with his left. Absent-mindedly he inclined his head to acknowledge to the crowd that they were there. He beckoned for the sword. "Is there a single principle I hold?" he asked. The crowd screamed at him. They wanted one pass more. He considered them. "Haven't I done enough?" he asked. The crowd cheered. He drew the bull. The bull passed him so close that although he did not fall his weight went on that left, that artificial, leg. The bull turned and he was off balance. He passed the bull on the left side and the bull caught him with its right horn, hooked and threw him. Lewis turned off the Generalísimo and went toward the racetrack. When he got onto the highway and was held up in the line of cars, he heaved himself off the ground, picked up his cape, waved the peons off, and took the bull all the way out to the center. In the parking lot he sat for a moment, keeping the attendant waiting while he passed the bull closer than ever before. Again on his right side. And as the attendant held out his hand for pesetas the bull hooked Lewis into the air on the right horn and when Lewis came down onto the ground the steel leg twisted beneath him; the bull gored Lewis again and again and again, and threw him again, the steel leg trailing after him, wherever he was thrown, by one twisted leather strap. "Here you are," said Lewis, handing over twenty-five pesetas.

At the races he couldn't lose. Whatever his system he picked the winner. He sat there gazing down at the long slim narrow pan shape, in the evening sunlight, under the glinting white arch, with children on the grass below, and fat women with artificial flowers in their ears, sat there urging on the Duke of Albuquerque.

"Much nicer crowd than at the bullfight," he said.

When he had won ten thousand pesetas he saw a girl in a blue

157

spotted dress with long blond hair and a red handbag. Lewis thought he might give her his winnings. He got up to do so but her companion came back. She took the man's arm, and smiled, so Lewis sat where he was.

The shadows stretched out and lay on the track.

The clouds went white and long and thin.

A helicopter flew over and startled the children.

At the last race Lewis picked a horse but didn't bet on it. He had now won fifteen thousand pesetas. Lewis simply sat where he was and waited for the race.

He could have been in England—the grass was so green.

There were thirteen horses for the mile. He watched the start through his binoculars, then stared at the blue hills while the horses made the turn. As they came to the finish his horse was leading easily when it put its foot in a hole and broke its leg. The jockey somersaulted and landed on his back. Lewis rubbed his eyes and stood up. But it was no dream. Lewis watched them pick up the jockey, he watched the horse stand with his head down, foot hanging on by a bit of thin flesh; Lewis saw the red bare bone. He waited until the vet came to inject, saw the horse fall into the hedge. He watched them fill up the hole. And even after all the people had gone, Lewis could not but sit there staring while they covered the horse with a green tarpaulin, and an old grey tractor came up with new ropes and hauled the dead animal off, past the winning post, over the scrub, and out the gate. Lewis sat there alone, then went to the parking lot and drove to Mexico Lindo's.

Slattery was not at Mexico Lindo's. Lewis waited an hour after the appointed time, drank beer, refused tequila.

He kept thinking about the dead horse. He tried to think of Vermont.

"What an awful last day I'm having," Lewis said.

He wished he could wander about in the rain in some green garden with box hedges and huge beds of flowers.

. . . . .

158

At eleven fifteen Lewis left the bar at Mexico Lindo's, got into the Alvis, and went back to the apartment with a parcel of hot *tacos* for himself and Slattery. Slattery was still working.

Lewis did not reproach him.

Lewis undid the *tacos,* served them up on a tray with a couple of cold beers.

Lewis told Slattery about the races while Slattery ate.

Slattery made no comment.

"He would have won, you see," said Lewis. "Poor thing."

"Yes," said Slattery and continued his work.

"I'll be glad to get out of here," Lewis said. "Out of Madrid."

Lewis was awakened by the sound of the doorbell. He turned on the light, looked at his watch. It was almost two.

The doorbell rang again.

Lewis got out of his bed, put on his silk robe, went to the door, and opened it.

It was a boy with a telegram. The telegram had *Urgente* written upon it. The telegram was addressed to Slattery.

Lewis tipped the boy, thanked the boy, shut the door, and went to Slattery's room. Lewis knocked on Slattery's bedroom door: there was no answer. Lewis went down the corridor to Slattery's studio room. Slattery was still working on his mother's head.

"Urgent telegram for you."

"What?"

"A telegram. It's marked urgent."

"Open it. Will ya?"

Lewis opened the telegram.

The telegram said: "Please phone me immediately." The telegram was signed by the doctor who had written to Slattery about his mother. The telegram gave a telephone number in Vermont.

Slattery put down his modeling tool, picked up a wet cloth out of a bucket of water, draped the cloth over the head, and took the telegram from Lewis.

"I can't do it. I can't use the phone. You do it for me."

159

"Will you come with me?"

"The *portero*'s got a phone."

"I'll stay here. I'll wait. I'll go to the kitchen and make us some coffee."

"All right," said Lewis. "We should get through very quickly at this time of night."

When Lewis came back Slattery was not in the kitchen. Slattery had drunk his coffee and was back in the studio again. Slattery had taken off the cloth and was working on his mother's head.

Sick and trembling, Lewis said: "I've spoken to the doctor."

"Yeah."

"I've spoken to the doctor . . . I have to tell you your mother's dead."

"Dead?"

"Yes."

"How dead?"

Lewis hesitated.

"Eh?"

Lewis realized he should have thought his story out.

"How?"

Confused, Lewis told the truth.

"She threw herself under a car."

"How could she do that?"

"Right in the grounds. Right in the driveway. With one of her nurses beside her. A delivery van. It wasn't even going fast."

"Was this after she knew I was comin'?" asked Slattery. "Had they told her that?"

12

Slattery waved a hand for the bill. The air was growing colder.

"They've given me ten days," said Slattery. "Ten days to pack up and clear out."

"Yes."

"I kicked a Spaniard; that's not allowed."

"I heard that."

"You should've gone with me, that night."

"You wouldn't let me, I tried."

"I can't remember it really," said Slattery. "I don't know where I ended up. In a brothel, I guess."

There were stars in the black sky above them, flowers in the floodlit grass.

"The whores here go by weight," said Slattery.

"I tried very hard to stop you," said Lewis. "But you weren't having any. Where will you go?"

Slattery did not answer. He gazed at the hills of lights.

"Where are you thinking of going?"

"They work on their backs with their legs in the air."

In the floodlight the undersides of the green leaves were white.

"Don't talk like that."

"What?"

"I don't like to hear you talk like that."

"You mean . . . you mean you still love your wife."

"Yes, I do," said Lewis.

The waiter arrived with the bill: Slattery paid it.

"You overtipped," said Lewis.

"So you still love your wife?"

161

"Yes. I've got an uncle at the Embassy, you know," said Lewis. "He might get someone to intercede for you . . . perhaps we could give some guarantees . . . I might be able in some way to . . ."

"What guarantees?" asked Slattery.

They looked at each other.

"I suppose you're right," said Lewis sadly. "So where will you go?"

"Tokyo."

"Tokyo?"

"How the hell do I know?"

"Well, I was wondering," said Lewis. "What I was wondering was whether we might . . ."

"Join forces?"

"Exactly," said Lewis. "Pool our assets."

"I don't know."

"You don't know."

"Maybe I was bad for ya."

"How do you mean?"

"Maybe."

"It wasn't your fault."

"No?"

"You did your best to dissuade me."

"Well, let's sleep on that," said Slattery, getting up. "Shall we go to a night club, Arthur?"

"A night club?"

"That's what I said."

There were dancing tapping ladies in white shoes and black hats.

"You still like women, Arthur."

There were girls with yellow flounces and knickers of black lace.

"One of 'em's got stickin' plaster on her thighs."

There were red knickers and blue knickers, there were mauves and oranges and greens.

"Maybe he told her he wouldn't let her out."

162

"What do you mean?"

"Maybe my father told my mother he wouldn't let her out."

"I don't think so," said Lewis.

"I do," said Slattery.

A girl began to dance with a castanet and a single braid.

"This place is like Lyon's Corner House," said Lewis.

"You don't think my father told my mother that?"

Nervously, but firmly, looking Slattery directly in the eyes, Lewis answered: "I most certainly do not."

A girl began to sing under a golden star. A girl with a page-boy cut. A girl in a beach dress with a muff around her knees. Between each verse of her song this singer gave a deliberate, neurotic twitch.

"Well, one thing's certain, isn't it?" said Slattery. "I can't go to Boston to find out."

A trumpeter blew with a twenties band.

"No, you can't," said Lewis.

On came electric guitars and pink girls in miniskirts.

"You indulge yourself too much," said Lewis.

The girls knelt down from the rostrum and presented them both with badges of palm trees.

"It's so respectable in here," said Slattery. "It's family night, so let's get out."

"What a warm floor it is," said Slattery. "You could lay down here on the floor with a woman and sunbathe!"

"What I want you to understand . . . what you must understand is that I wanted to see that look on her face."

"There are more old women here than anywhere in the world," said Slattery.

"I wanted to see that look of pleasure on her face. That's how much I loved her."

"Here," said Slattery, "they'll go with sixty-fives and seventy-fives. That's what the gigolos will do. In New York forty-five's the top."

"I would have stood at a window to see that look of pleasure on her face."

"In Madrid," said Slattery, "it's young boys and widows. No shame to it."

"I would have looked over any man's shoulders to see that look of pleasure on Jean's face."

"No embarrassment here," said Slattery. "Husband's always home by eleven. Never lunches with the wife. The wife's lover's always young. Seven till nine. Madrid's the city of beautiful chauffeurs. Madrid's the city for fuckin' in cars."

"You don't seem to understand," said Lewis. "Not to participate. Not always to have to participate. But just to see that beautiful look."

"When she comes, you mean?"

"Yes," said Lewis. "That is what I mean. Why does one always have to participate?"

"Have you ever noticed how everybody's dyin' for an exit?" asked Slattery. "Have you ever noticed how the men age in Spain? Never get any sleep. It's only the old and the children take siestas. Not the lovers."

"I must begin all over again," said Lewis. "I must find another."

"All Negroes should be Negroes; that's what he told me. Old man Boston. All Jews Jews. Old man Boston. Any nigger tried to go to bed with him, he says no . . . that's his standard! Cocktails okay! But no nigger lays him. He may let them hold his old dicky . . . while he pisses . . . but that's all. Old man Boston."

"My mother was the most wonderful woman."

"Old man dicky swingin' in his uniform with a great black prick up his ass."

"My mother loved me. Love does relieve loneliness."

"The blacker the nigger," said Slattery, "the better I love them. That's what I told my father."

"Another Jean," said Lewis.

They staggered into the warm narrow beautiful streets with the boxes of flowers outside the windows. They left the tired old whores still testing their gins and guessing. They left the Mar

164

Blanca, the Tu-yo and the Eva. The black sky was above them. The stars had disappeared. They reeled between the Lambrettas and the white-pistoled soldiers. They waved to the old women on the balconies above—the old women muttering down at them like quarrelsome angels. They had kissed the hands of hat-check girls. They had said good-bye forever to the shampooed whores —to the "ten-pesetas-a-combing, well-coiffed Spanish whores" —to the "pulling-up-their-dresses, thinking-they'd-make-a-conquest, gold-dusted" Spanish whores—to the "too-fuckin'-fat-for-me-to-handle-Arthur" Spanish whores—to the "all-with-illegitimate-children" Spanish whores.

"Madrid people are cat people. We should have electric dicks."

"I would have liked to have fucked her on a rooftop, Patrick."

They went home to pack.

13

The packing was almost done but they needed more rope.

"It's got to be Africa. It's got to be Tunis."

"Well."

"You stay on till the lease is up while I go look."

"Yes."

"When I've found somethin' I'll send for the stuff. If an Arab does me in you keep it."

"Are you sending for me also?"

"Only you can answer that question."

"Hmm."

"Why don't you get a lousy job?"

"Puritan," said Lewis.

"My will's in your favor," said Slattery.

They found an old rope shop in a curve of the Calle Toledo. It was double-fronted with tiny windows displaying every variety of rope. On the window sills piles of rope sandals. The inside of the shop smelled of hessian dust and dried weeds. There was a tangle of raffia dropping from a beam in the ceiling; there were six-foot piles of sacking in the corners. On the shelves more sandals. They went to the back of the shop. Behind the counter there were paper rolls. A small corridor led to the dusty storage room.

"That's what I want," said Slattery, pointing.

Slattery went to the coil, lifted an end, ran it through his fingers.

"This is the most suitable for hanging," Slattery said.

Frowning, Lewis inquired the price.

"It's called Mudeja de Caniama," said Slattery. "I'll pay. I've gotta get rid of pesetas. How much?"

"Ten feet for fifty," answered the frowning Lewis.

Outside, Lewis asked, "What kind of job?"

"Social work. Old men should get social."

"I'm not old!"

"Why do you act it then?"

"Do I?"

"You could've laid her as well now as when you were twenty. Better. You could've been layin' her at eighty."

"Oh you don't understand," said Lewis. "You haven't the remotest comprehension."

"Who does?"

They got into the Alvis and went to Alducino's.

"What a clientele," said Lewis.

"Who's talkin'!"

"Exactly," said Lewis. "Something's got to be done with me. All these foreign dregs."

The light was dim. The wood panels were dark and thin—on these panels groups of film actors praised the spaghetti.

"I've gotta leave ya. I've gotta take a last look round."

"Don't get into any trouble."

The fans above their heads were noisy.

"No, I've gotta do my last shoppin'. I might go down the Rastro."

"Shall I come?"

"I've got to wander. I've gotta say good-bye."

"I understand."

The eternal students entered the restaurant.

"Jesus," said Slattery. "I'm off. Have a siesta."

Lewis remained to finish his brandy.

The students sang:

> "She left with another
> And here I remain."

"Oh Christ, just my luck," said Lewis.

Shall I too say good-bye to Madrid? wondered Lewis.

. . . . .

167

Once or twice during his troubled siesta Lewis half woke and thought he heard doors opening and closing and Slattery's footsteps passing his door and going down the long corridor, but on each occasion he wrenched himself back into his dreams again and turned over onto his stomach.

"Are ya gonna sleep all night?"

"Mmm."

"Are ya gonna sleep all night?"

Slattery was shaking him.

"What's the matter?"

"It's after seven."

"What?"

"It's after seven."

"Is it?"

"You gonna get up?"

"Yes."

"I'll fix you a drink."

Slattery left the room.

Lewis stretched his arms, shook himself, and got up.

When Lewis entered the drawing room he asked: "Whatever did happen to that boy who was sleeping on the sofa?"

"Killed himself."

Slattery handed Lewis a cup of coffee and a glass of brandy.

"You never told me."

"What was the point?"

"Here?"

"No, New York. Went back there. That did it."

"Oh dear," said Lewis.

"Nobody rang the doorbell when I was out?"

"I didn't hear anyone."

"I left a message with the *portero*. He said nobody called."

"Are you expecting somebody then?"

"Somebody might wanna say good-bye. Somebody might. What's the time?"

Lewis looked at his watch. "Almost half past."

"Seven?"

"Yes, seven."

"Jesus, you must have slept for hours," said Slattery.

Lewis sipped his brandy.

"How'd your shopping go?"

"I got you a present."

Slattery went to the sideboard and brought back a parcel.

"How very kind of you."

"Open it."

Lewis did so.

Inside the parcel was a carved nude figure of a young girl—a girl in black ebony.

"Pretty, ain't it?"

"It's beautiful."

"I thought you'd like it. I reckon she's twelve."

"Thank you very much."

"Don't mention it," said Slattery.

They drank.

"Done all your packing?"

"All but the pictures. I haven't roped my pictures."

"Can I help you?"

"No, I'll do that myself. What's the time now?"

"I just told you. It's about twenty-five to eight."

They drank.

"I'll come with you to the airport."

"There's no need."

"I'd like to come."

"Okay. Soon as I get somewhere I'll let you know."

"I'd appreciate that."

They drank.

Lewis put his nude girl on the mantelpiece.

"D'you want to go out?"

"No."

"I thought you might want to have a last jar in one of your favorites."

"If I do that I miss anyone who calls."

"We could leave a message."

"No, I like it here. We'll stay here just in case."

"All right."

169

"Nobody comes by one o'clock we'll go out drinkin'."

How odd, thought Lewis. If it were my last night in Madrid I'd be sure to go out, thought Lewis. I'd go out now.

"I'm leaving you my pictures."

"Yes."

"They might be worth something some day."

"How d'you mean, exactly?"

"I've made a list for you. I've catalogued the pictures. Here."

Slattery took a folded paper out of his jacket pocket, handed it to Lewis.

"Thank you."

"If the pictures are good, that justifies everythin'."

"What?"

"If the pictures are good, I rest in peace."

"What are you talking about?"

"If a man's work has meanin', it don't matter about his life."

"I don't agree with that at all," said Lewis. "You're just as important to me whether you paint well or not."

"I am?"

"Of course."

"Really?"

"If you were the worst painter who ever lived I wouldn't give a damn."

"You mean it?"

"It's you that matters to me," said Lewis. "Not your bloody work."

"That's not how the world thinks."

"Anyway," said Lewis, "I know you can paint."

They drank.

"I must make you another catalogue."

"What?"

"A catalogue of women for you."

"What?"

"Put their names and phone numbers. Put checks against possibles. Stars against probables. Some of 'em you may know. Those you know and don't fancy you'd cross out."

"What?"

170

"A list of potentials."

"I can find women for myself you know!" Lewis was indignant.

"Look, Arthur," said Slattery, pouring himself another brandy, "I could make you a list of fifteen women and every one of 'em would take you for a husband."

"They would?"

"Every one of 'em could love you."

"You think so? Are they all American?"

"They're all American. They've been punished."

"Well, I don't know," said Lewis doubtfully, "I think you're mocking me."

"Arthur," said Slattery, "I was never more serious in my life. For Christ's sake take unto yourself some poor unfortunate woman who's been ravaged, bit, sneered at, plundered, and redeem her. Take a poor American who's been gnawed, take her to your flat old bosom and restore her."

"Well . . ."

"I wanna look down and see you a grandfather. Give me your pen."

"Oh Christ," said Lewis, "you can't go on that plane tomorrow. You can't. Let's get pissed. I don't want you to go on that plane tomorrow."

The doorbell rang.

"They aren't all American, Arthur. One of 'em's called Cynthia. And there's Mavis. And a couple of Swedes."

"I see."

"There's a lot of women in Madrid."

The doorbell rang again.

"Go to Switzerland and get yourself an injection, Arthur."

Rising, Lewis said: "I'll see who it is."

"What's the time?"

"Five past eight."

"Yeah, see who it is," said Slattery, and thrust out his hand. Surprised, Lewis took it.

"I hate good-byes."

"Yes."

171

"So I'm sayin' it now."

"All right. Good-bye."

"Good-bye."

"After our guest's gone we'll go down to the *alemana*."

"All right."

The doorbell rang long and insistently.

"We'll go down there after he's gone."

Lewis let go Slattery's hand, left the room, crossed the hall-way, and opened the door. On the step stood a frail old man with a crew cut, wearing a white raincoat.

"Good evening."

"Good evening," answered Lewis.

"Does Patrick Slattery live here?"

"Yes, he does."

"Is he dead?"

"What?"

"I asked you if he's dead."

"No, he's not dead. Of course he's not dead."

"May I come in?"

Lewis nodded his head: the old man entered, stood in the hallway and took off his coat.

"I'm his father."

Lewis took the coat.

"How do you do. I'm Arthur Lewis."

"Larry Slattery."

Lewis took the old man's coat and hung it up.

"He's in the living room. I'll show you. May I go first?"

"Yeah. Do that."

Lewis led the way down the hall to the living room. The door was open.

"Patrick," said Lewis, "your father's come to see you."

But the room was empty.

"Come in, will you, please," said Lewis. "Patrick was here a moment ago. Do sit down and I'll go and find him. Would you like a drink?"

"I don't drink."

"A cup of coffee then?"

"No, wait a minute."

Lewis paused in the doorway.

"Come here, son."

"Yes."

"Come here, son."

Lewis returned to the middle of the room.

"You say he was in this room?"

"Yes."

"When the doorbell rang?"

"Yes."

"Then why's he gone out?"

"I don't know."

"Why's he gone out?"

"I don't know. Perhaps he's gone to the bathroom or something."

"Perhaps. He's a joker, ain't he?"

The old man put his hand into his jacket pocket.

"He was always a joker."

The old man took out a sheaf of telegrams.

"He sent us these. I was the only one could come. His sisters. His brothers. The President. The Mayor of Boston. The Strangler. Sent that one to the asylum. A psychiatrist he knew. Some old high-school friends . . . guys he used to run with. His aunt. A lawyer. The doctor where his mother died. And me. Sent them all greetings. And his wife."

"His wife?"

"That's what I said."

The old man held out the telegrams.

"Take one, they're all the same."

Lewis took one of the telegrams.

"Did ya know about this?"

"I did not."

"Read it then."

Lewis put on his glasses.

"He might be jokin' or he might be doin' it now."

173

Lewis read: "Friday is my last day on earth. Friday night I shall hang myself with my paintings." The telegram was signed: Patrick Slattery with love.

"Is he jokin'?"

"Joking?"

"Where's his studio?"

"Stay here," shouted Lewis. "Stay here." Lewis turned and began to run.

Lewis pounded down the long corridor to the studio shouting out, "Patrick! Patrick! Don't do it, Patrick."

Lewis reached the studio door and flung it open.

Swinging in a corner of the room, dressed in a policeman's uniform, his young mother's head in his arms, was Patrick Slattery. The feet twirled north, south, east, and west. The great protruding eyes gleamed, and centered upon Lewis as if in eternal reproach.

Lewis screamed.

A spot lamp was trained on the corpse.

The corpse twirled and the brass buttons glittered in all the mirrors.

The peak of the cap flashed in the mirrors.

Lewis stood. Then he saw it was a dummy. A dummy in an American policeman's uniform with Slattery's own clay head on top.

"Patrick!"

Silence.

"Where are you, Patrick?"

Slattery stood up from behind the packing cases.

"Where is he?"

"Your father?"

"Why didn't ya bring him?"

"You're mad."

"Go and get him. Tell him I've done it. Go and get him or you'll spoil it."

"You're mad."

"For Christ's sake go and get the old bastard and let's see his face in the mirrors. Tell him I'm hanged."

174

"No."

"I haven't got all this rigged for nothin'. It's taken me hours. Look at those screws. I've gone to a lot of trouble to get all this. Cost me a lot of pesetas. Cost me a lot of passion."

"You miserable shit," said Lewis, and began to shake.

"He killed my mother, didn't he?"

"You miserable shit," said Lewis. "He's the only one who's come here. I don't like you. I don't like you at all. Why didn't you tell me you were going to do this, you miserable dishonest self-pitying cruel bastard. You sick self-indulgent bastard . . ."

"Swings well, don't it?" said Slattery giving the dummy a push. "For Christ's sake get my father!"

Lewis thrust Slattery violently out of the way, picked up the mallet, and battered at the heads and the dummy. The head of the mother fell on the floor.

"Don't do that. He should've let her out!"

"You miserable shit, I'll have this right down from here. And you're going to apologize. That's what you're going to do. I'm not having any of this. I'm not having any of this at all."

"You're not?"

"You could have killed him with the shock of it."

"I could."

"And me too! He's an old man. He's a frail old man."

Slattery started to laugh.

"Fooled *you*, didn't I? Got ya, didn't I, Arthur?"

"It's not funny," said Lewis, battering away with the mallet. "It's not funny at all."

"I'm sorry."

"You're not sorry. You're never sorry. You'll never change. You're a self-pitying, self-destructive lying bastard. And what about your wife? You never told me that either."

"I didn't?"

"I wouldn't trust you as far as I could throw you," said Lewis.

Lewis put his arms round the dummy and heaved: the noose remained but the body came crashing to the floor. And so did

175

the other head. Both heads were cracked and broken on the floor.

"All that remains of my handiwork," said Slattery. "Poor things."

"You kept it all from me, didn't you?"

"All right, get the old man."

"You kept it all from me. *You're* no friend."

"Get the old man, for Christ's sake, and let's have a drink."

"He doesn't drink. No, you're no friend!"

Lewis put his hand on his beating heart.

"Well, we can give him a Coca-Cola. We can give him a Coca-fuckin'-Cola, can't we, for Christ's sake?"

For Lewis, out of the shock, came rage.

"And anyway," said Lewis, "your mother knew you were coming. Your father had nothing to do with that. I didn't tell you, to spare your feelings. Your mother knew you were coming to see her before she killed herself. Her doctor told me that. Her doctor told me he'd told her that that very afternoon."

Lewis stared at Slattery.

"Consider that," said Lewis. "You just think about that. I'm not sparing your feelings any longer."

Lewis turned his back on Slattery and left the studio.

"I heard ya shoutin'!" said the old man.

"Yes."

"I heard ya shoutin'. I'd have come but I figured I'm not as strong as I was. Is he all right?"

"Yes, he's all right."

"He was jokin', was he?"

"You could call it that."

"You told him off."

"In a way."

"That won't do any good."

"No."

"Tellin' my boy off never did him any good," said the old man.

"He wants to see you."

"He does?"

176

"Yes."

"You're sure?"

"Yes."

"Okay," said the old man. "Comin'?"

"No."

"I'd be obliged if you'd come."

"No."

"I haven't seen him in years . . . you'd be a help to me."

"I'm going out," said Lewis. "I lost my temper. I went too far . . . he frightened me so much."

"Please," said the old man.

Lewis stopped.

"Please," said the old man. "Please."

Lewis took off his coat.

14

Lewis lifted the briefcase onto the counter, turned to shake hands.

"This is as far as I can go," Lewis said.

"Thank you," answered the old man.

Embarrassed they dropped their eyes.

"He *was* his mother's favorite, you know," said the old man, raising his head.

"Yes."

"If you hear from him, let me know."

"Yes."

"I enjoyed your company."

The old man went through the barrier without looking back.

Coming out of the airport Lewis took a side road and drove away north of Madrid. The road was still wet after the thunderstorm, pools of water lay at its side in the yellow mud, lank poppies stood up in the corn, a red-headed partridge ate in the laced tall grass.

Lewis drove deeper into the valley.

Over the flowers hung a low wet mist. Lewis stopped the car and got out. He walked away from the road into the broom and the foxgloves.

Magpies jumped up into the poplars like monkeys.

Rabbits ran into a clump of umbrella pines.

Ahead of him lay scythed hay, cornflowers, black cattle, mules, donkeys, and a stone cross.

Blanketed old men and women sat at the grey cross watching the cows.

Lewis walked toward them and sat down also where the

broom grew over the rocks like seaweed, and the purple foxgloves like sea pinks, sat down beside a hairy white donkey
whose back was covered in thistledown, watched a crane walk
slowly toward him on its long red legs.

Lewis stopped at the florist's on the corner and bought a
flowering plant in a pot. He placed the pot carefully on the floor
behind the passenger seat, got back into the car, and drove on.

Lewis drove through the middle of Madrid, went out of the
city past the Toledo gate, over the Toledo bridge, over the Manzanares.

"Deaf-man's villa," Lewis remembered.

The road was torn up except for the trolley lines. The Alvis
creaked and bumped. They were laying new gaspipes. There
were bricks, black water, and floating newspapers in the torn-up
gutters.

Two or three times the bottom of the Alvis hit the broken
surface. Lewis worried about the oil sump.

A hearse passed him, going the opposite direction, back into
Madrid—a black baroque old-fashioned hearse with horse
lamps.

At the top of the lanes of dried mud he could see the little
cemetery.

He climbed the narrow lane that circled round the wall, came
to the gate, stopped the Alvis, took up his plant, got out, went to
the door, and rang the bell. The old woman opened up and he
entered.

"*Gracias. Gracias.*"

Inside the walls, the flowers smelled sweet. There was a
child's doll on marble and grey granite. Lewis stepped over the
black hoses and went down the path.

There was ivy on Squadron Leader Caldwell's grave—*Squadron Leader Caldwell 1944—died aged forty-three.*

Here between the formal trees, in the shadow of the mausoleum, the light was dimmer.

The British Embassy Church of St. George, said the notice
board. *Please do not touch the trees or plants. If you consider*

179

that a grave could be better maintained please consult the care-
taker about it.

On his left: *Miss Forrester was inhumated here.* On his right:
John and Alda Donovan of Dublin R.I.P.

Lewis continued around the bend in the stone path carrying
his potted plant. He passed a wheelbarrow and a cluster of old
women in black brushing up leaves and pulling ivy off tombstones. Beyond them other old women in black were raking the
leaves into neat piles among tombstones and trees.

Baroness Tatiana de Korff
1891 Born St. Petersburg
1961 Died Madrid.

Good company for her I hope, thought Lewis.

He went by thorn trees with red berries and one of the
branches reached out and caught the sleeve of his jacket.

A cross lay on its side by a headless angel.

All he could hear within these walls was the raking of the
leaves.

He crossed through a patch of sunlight, passed through an
arch, and here on the other side once again it was shaded and
the trees were old and dusty.

Here there was a plumber at work irrigating the flowers, and a
grandchild sat alone on a stack of tiled bricks.

His mother's grave looked grey and much used.

Lewis put down his plant.

Lewis brushed the leaves off the grey stone with his hands.

All Lewis could hear was the raking of the leaves, all he could
smell was the burning of the leaves in the piles.

White clouds passed overhead in the blue sky.

Lewis beckoned.

Lewis beckoned to an old woman in black.

"Keep it tidy," he said, giving her a five-hundred-peseta note.
"Keep it tidy, *por favor.*"

"Only the keepers from now on."

"The keepers?"

"Only room for the keepers from now on," she said. "My

180

husband will be the last," the old woman said. "My son, Primavera, is there already."

Lewis went back past the cold white chapel—past the marble catafalque—with the stained British crowns on the windows, and the old women washing the red-and-white floor.

Outside on the cobbles it was much warmer. Below him was a grave for cars. Below him boys fought with sticks. Below him were television antennas on every slum.

Lewis leaned against the Alvis and took out a cigar.

He had no idea what to do, or where to go next.

Beyond the slums there were domes.

On the cemetery wall, *Prohibido Hacer.*

"Don't piss: five-hundred-pesetas fine," as Slattery would have said.

In the doorways of the slums girls sat on chairs with their hair in curlers reading magazines. There were women and cats and babies sitting on the dirt.

To the north there were larger cemeteries—cemeteries with great trimmed hedges and huge marble vaults.

There too they were burning the leaves.

Lewis looked at his mother's cemetery; his mother's cemetery must be the smallest in Madrid.

The sky darkened. The wind blew dust around him. The girls on the chairs went inside.

Lewis got into the Alvis and drove back down the winding mud lane onto the road.

Lewis was sitting alone in the apartment one afternoon, waiting for the lease to run out, when a postcard was pushed through the mail slot. He went into the hall and picked it up. He put on his glasses and took it to the sunshine. He poured himself a drink and sat down on the balcony.

On the front of the postcard a camel drank beside a date palm. On the back was a list of women's names, and phone numbers. Some of the names had checks beside them, some of the names had stars.

181

Lewis put down the card and stood up. He went to the balcony rail. He looked down.

He picked up the card again. There was no address. The postmark was Morocco.

Lewis finished his drink.

Lewis poured himself another.

Then Lewis took the card, went down to the *portero,* and telephoned the first name that had a star beside it.